STOLEN SHADOW BRIDE

STOLEN BRIDES OF THE FAE

S.M. GAITHER

For Grant—
Because I love you even more than I love broody fae princes.

PROLOGUE

A BARGAIN OF SHADOW AND SUN

*T*here once were two princesses when there only should have been one.

Two sisters conceived during a Hunter's moon, just as their mother had been, and her mother before her, and her mother before her... and on and on it went, all the way back to the moment the bargain had been struck between the rulers of the human kingdom of Middlemage and the fae lands to the east and west of that kingdom.

For generations—because of that ancient bargain— it had been this way: Always twins. Always marked. One by Shadow. One by Sun. One destined to stay. One destined for the fae.

The one that stayed eventually became the ruler of Middlemage.

The one that went away to the fae lands became... something else.

The children's fates were intertwined with that of their human kingdom and those neighboring fae lands;

the first twin saw the rule of the Caster family and its bloodline continued, uninterrupted, while the spare child was given as a gift to one of those two fae courts, alternating between them with each new generation.

For over a century, it continued like this, each set of twins a renewed and living, breathing symbol of balance and peace.

But Sephia and Leanora Caster were different.

They were marked as clearly as any before them: The firstborn, Sephia, was Shadow. Nora was Sun. Sephia was destined to stay and rule as Middlemage's queen. Nora was destined to be stolen away by the Court of the Sun, as it was their turn, their privilege, their *right* to take her.

This was the way the story had gone for so long that all other possible outcomes for the girls' lives had been forgotten, cast aside.

That is not how this story goes.

It was more twisted than this from the very beginning.

Sephia should have died, the doctors said, because she had been born with a heart too small and too weak to sustain her life. If she had been any other child—a normal human child not infused with the magic that had come about as part of that ancient fae bargain— then she would have died.

There should have only been one princess who lived.

But Sephia was not a normal human child, and so Sephia lived.

And perhaps because of the shadowy fae magic that filled in the weak and empty spaces of her heart, she grew up wild and a touch wicked, and the people of the capital city of Ocalith rarely dared to speak ill of her unless they were clutching a cluster of verbena flowers or an iron cross for protection, and they averted their eyes and recited prayers under their breath whenever royal processions with her in them passed by.

How? The people whispered in between their clutching and praying. *How can a girl with such a shadowy heart become our peaceful ruler some day?*

Still, perhaps more disturbing than the heir was the spare. The younger sister, Nora, who had been born healthy enough, grew strange and sickly as the years passed. Her straw-colored hair took on the actual texture of straw. Her skin developed a grey tint to it, along with premature wrinkling.

Elephant Princess, the cruelest of the village children hissed behind her back.

And the fae magic that should have been Nora's never manifested in any noticeable way.

She should have held at least some dominion over the light and warmth of the natural world. Instead, rumors claimed that her eyes were truly pitch black—you'd see this for yourself if you looked directly into them—and that she didn't sleep most nights, that she ate her meat mostly raw and bloody, that her hands constantly shook, that walking became increasingly difficult for her as she aged...

There were those who said that Sephia— weak, half-hearted Sephia— had lived because she had stolen her younger sister's magic. This was what had ruined Nora. What was slowly killing her, even.

Nora knew better; her elder sister was her keeper, not her killer.

But people outside of a family looking into it rarely understood the whole truth of things.

They saw a quiet girl who looked strange, who did not have the magic and the beauty and the strength a princess should have, and so came whispers: *The girl is ruined. What happens to us when we try to give her away, as the law demands? It could mean war. Our kingdom will suffer for it, either way.*

They would suffer, they reasoned, because the fae on either side did not take kindly to ruined gifts.

As Sephia grew older, she learned of the brutal, terrifying sort of things that the fae did with gifts that they did not take kindly to, and her once-weak heart grew ever stronger with the desire to protect her little sister from those brutal things.

And so, on the eve of their thirteenth birthday, Sephia began to plot.

In eight years, the fae would come to claim Nora as a wife for their youngest prince.

In eight years, Sephia would be ready for them. She would take her sister's place. *Somehow*, she would take her place.

And if the kingdom suffered for it, then so be it.

CHAPTER 1

8 Years Later

Sephia pushed her way through the trees, clutching a bottle of putrid-smelling liquid to her chest.

There were no birds flittering about. No rabbits scurrying nor deer bounding away from the crown princess's frantic steps. The air smelled of honeysuckle and smoke and sea salt, all mingled together, all being carried in on an unnaturally warm wind that tingled with the faint energy of magic. The trees seemed to stretch and reach out for that wind as it brushed through them, as though trying to wrap the magic around their branches and keep it for themselves—

All signs that further twisted up Sephia's already anxious stomach.

The Court of the Sun would arrive within the hour, she suspected.

She ran faster. Across the rocky hills and through the

massive forest that encircled the town of Ocalith. Past the shrines where villagers came to lay offerings to their fae neighbors. Over clear streams edged with ice. Winter had arrived earlier than usual this year, and Sephia's feet felt partially frozen despite the warm winds of magic and the fur lining of her boots. Every pounding step stung.

Finally, the trees around her thinned. She caught a glimpse of the afternoon sky, bright as a robin's egg. A faint sliver of white was the only mark against the otherwise clear canvas.

The moon.

"It's visible so early..." she muttered to herself.

Another bad omen.

As though the impending disaster needed any *omens* to herald it. Everyone knew it was happening. For months, it had been all the people of Ocalith could talk about.

Sephia pushed on, making her way into the agreed-upon clearing.

Just ahead, Nora was waiting for her beneath the sycamore tree that had often served as a center point of their childhood games. They had carved faces and words and wishes into the grey bark of that tree, fashioned knotted ropes and crude swings to hang from its sprawling branches.

Nana Rosa had been *furious* during the only occasion when she'd actually caught the two of them climbing and swinging from one of the highest of those branches; Sephia could almost hear the old woman's shrill voice echoing through the clearing, even now.

A fine thing it would be for one of you two to break your

neck doing something so foolish—as if you don't already worry your parents enough!

Nora had stuck to the lower branches after that scolding.

Sephia had found a way to climb higher, just to prove to herself that she could do it without getting caught.

It had been four years since Nora had been strong enough to climb anything.

But Sephia still occasionally helped her sister onto one of the lower swings, secured her hold on the frayed rope handles, and then sent her flying with a gentle push. There was something about leaning back in a swing, the sky rising and falling above you, hair dusting the ground...something that always made both of the sisters forget about their weaknesses and pains. About their obligations and the dangerous, uncertain futures that awaited them.

Nora stood just to the right of one of those crooked swings now, wearing a dress the color of a calm sea. Her back was to Sephia. The train of the dress cascaded down, fluid and shimmering in the sunlight as though it actually *had* been fashioned from the blue-green waves of the Loral Sea.

The dress's delicate fabric and endlessly billowing skirts seemed out of place in this wild and frozen forest. But it was befitting of the future wife of a young fae prince—and there would be no time to go back to the palace before they met that prince.

It would be impossible to fly while wearing that, Sephia thought, her gaze flickering to the swing beside her sister.

She pulled her thoughts away from childhood games

7

and swept a cautious look around the edges of the clearing. Then she stepped forward, making no sound until her boot cracked a fallen limb a few feet away from Nora.

Nora spun around, clutching toward the small of her back. It was out of habit; she normally kept a dagger there. Her forest-green eyes were bright with a fear that settled quickly once she recognized her sister. Her gaze softened, and she pulled her hand away from her back as she asked, "You have it?"

"Yes. Sorry it took me so long."

"It's okay. We'll just have to move quickly." Nora's tone was gentle, but the lack of her usual smile betrayed her true concern.

Sephia breathed in deep, steadying herself.

She would have obtained the potion she held long before now, but the witch she'd bargained with had insisted that it wouldn't keep; the initial spell needed fresh blood, and it needed to be used within moments of adding that blood. They had considered taking care of this spell days ago, but the chances of their trickery being detected within their own familiar palace was too great.

So it all had to be done at the last minute, here in the quiet and secret of the forest.

It was not ideal.

Their parents would no doubt have realized they were missing by this point. The procession would be gathering at the palace gates, preparing to head for *Tala Nofa*, that great pavilion edged with fluttering flags and towering statues—a space that stood as yet another monument to the bargain that had been struck over a century ago. They would all be readying themselves for the ceremonial *Taking* that would occur there.

The king and queen would be livid over their daughters' late arrival to such an earth-shatteringly important event. Reasonably so; it was offensive to be late, after all.

And to offend the fae was to risk the lives and limbs of everyone within that royal procession.

But it couldn't be helped. Sephia had accepted this. They would just have to hurry back and try to smooth things over and minimize the damage.

Quickly, quickly...

Sephia clamped her teeth around the bottle's cork stopper and yanked. The smell that wafted out was as potent as it had been in that witch's house—like a cross between horse dung and vinegar with a hint of grass clippings.

She was not looking forward to drinking it.

But she didn't hesitate. She pulled two small cups and two glass vials from the satchel at her side. Knelt down, placed these things on the partially-frozen ground. Distributed one-fourth of the foul potion evenly between the cups. Yanked the small hunting knife from the sheath hidden at her ankle.

Her blade flew over her palm so quickly, so methodically, that she didn't have time to flinch.

Blood bubbled up over her skin. She scooped as much as she could into one of the glass vials, and then she wiped the remnants on a scraggly patch of grass, grabbed the still-empty vial, and stood to meet her sister's gaze.

"Give me your hand," she said.

S.M. GAITHER

Nora hesitated. Not likely from fear; she simply had a habit of taking her time with important things. They had always been this way: Nora was the calm inhale, the bracing breath before the storm. Sephia was the exhale, the wind that stirred the waves and pushed things—often violently— into motion.

And it was Sephia that moved more quickly this time, too. She firmly took Nora's wrist in her grip and pulled her forward.

Her blade moved as fast as before.

The blood oozed out to be collected. Once she was satisfied with the amount she'd gathered, she shook a drop from each of the vials into each of the cups. They landed with an oddly loud *plop* into the liquid.

That liquid spell sizzled. Its scent grew more overwhelming. Sephia held her breath as she grabbed the cups and handed one to her sister.

"Cheers," Nora said with a nervous little laugh.

They drank.

The forest seemed to grow even more abnormally quiet as the liquid burned down Sephia's throat.

She blinked, and suddenly the color leached from the trees, from the sky, from the dress Nora wore. Deep shadows stretched over their surroundings—shadows that didn't seem to follow any normal patterns, that were brought about by something unrelated to the cold sunlight. Sephia closed her eyes, hoping it would all be over with quickly.

When she blinked those eyes open a few minutes later, she was greeted by the sight of... *herself*.

No, not herself; this was now her sister, somehow.

The spell had *worked.*

"Incredible," Nora whispered, her eyes trailing over Sephia's transformed appearance. After a moment, her hands reached up and felt along her own altered face. "And I...do I..."

"I put a mirror in my bag—*your* bag, now." Sephia slipped that bag off her shoulder and handed it over. "See for yourself."

Nora pulled the mirror out, and Sephia stared at Nora as Nora stared at her new reflection. They had never been identical, and as they'd grown older they had resembled each other less and less, and so the changes were difficult to look away from.

The young woman who stood before Sephia now was no longer straw-haired and green-eyed. Instead, she had Sephia's own wavy, medium-length black locks. Her eyes were the palest shade of blue imaginable—like chips of ice, Nana Rosa had always said. Even the scar that ran along Sephia's hand—the result of a careless bit of knife work during one of her many cooking lessons with Chef Talos—had been transferred in exact detail.

Sephia's stomach gave a little lurch.

This was terrifyingly powerful magic.

Worse, it was magic that she did not fully trust nor understand, despite the countless hours she'd spent studying and preparing for this moment. If she had not been so desperate to take her sister's place, to protect her, then she never would have dared to set foot in that witch's domain.

Love could make one face all kinds of terrifying things, she supposed.

For better or worse.

That oddly warm breeze stirred the trees once more, reminding her of the *fae* magic that she needed to be more concerned with. That witch's strange spell was over and done with.

Now comes the hard part, and I need to stay focused.

They undressed and then redressed in each other's clothing, teeth chattering and skin pebbling all the while. Sephia took great care to not let any part of the ceremonial dress trail through the dirt, to not scuff her shoes, to not let her cut palm drip blood on anything. She even took a moment to pull her hair into a neat bun and secure it with the pins Nora had brought along with her; Nora would never have appeared before any royal processions looking anything other than her best.

And she was Nora now.

She wrapped her cut hand in a thin bandage before slipping Nora's delicate gloves on, and then she smoothed her skirts while the real Nora, looking enviously comfortable in Sephia's own trousers and an elegant but simple coat, went back to studying her reflection in the mirror.

"I know it isn't the point of all of this," Nora said. "It's just nice to be beautiful for once."

Sephia frowned. "You were beautiful before."

Nora shrugged, a wistful smile playing across her lips, her gaze still locked on her new reflection.

How strange to see my smile through someone else's eyes, Sephia thought.

"I still believe you got the worse end of the deal," Nora insisted.

"Hardly." Sephia grinned. "This time tomorrow, you'll

be sitting in one of Master Sonja's history lessons, bored to tears, while I'll be off on a new adventure."

Nora's smile remained, though it looked more forced now.

Neither of them dared to bring up the details of what that *adventure* might entail.

"Come on," Sephia said, tucking away the leftover potion and the vial of Nora's blood before heading down a narrow trail that led to their tied horses. "We need to hurry, as you said."

Approaching those horses was the first test of their transformation spell.

Sephia moved toward Daisy—Nora's horse—slowly, watching for signs that the creature might be confused, or that she might spook. But Daisy only regarded the transformed Sephia with a lazy look, and with a swish of her braided tail she went back to ripping up clumps of the frozen grass.

Nora approached Sephia's old mare with similar results.

"It's working as expected," Nora commented. She sounded awestruck all over again by what they'd done, though it *was* expected; the witch's potion changed outward appearances. It altered their energies. Their scents. Their voices. Their *everything*, almost— though the witch had warned that movements and habits could not be completely disguised, and neither could any illnesses or innate magics that ran too deeply.

So it was enough to trick the horses, but it could not fully hide Sephia's Shadow magic. Nor could it disguise the way Nora's hands shook, or the weakness that occasionally overtook the younger twin's steps.

That shakiness was one of the only *true* rumors about Nora that existed within the endless, cruel stream of them; she truly *had* been growing weaker as the years passed. Sicker—and from an ailment that no doctor had been able to name. Her hands trembled even now, as she worked to shove the mirror back into the leather satchel.

That trembling could give them away, Sephia knew.

It made this plan all the more dangerous.

But it was also the very thing that had driven her to take Nora's place: She was not going to send her feeble little sister into the clutches of monsters.

The fae were mysterious in many ways, but Sephia knew enough about them to know that they would not treat a sick human with kindness. There was nothing in the bargain struck all of those centuries ago that required them to do so.

They always came with the same plan, and it didn't involve *niceties*: They took the spare twin as their bride, coupled with them to fully awaken their own magic, and after that...

After that, it was said that they killed their wives as often as they kept them.

And if the rumors about Prince Tarron were true, his bride would be lucky to last a month.

They were all ruthless, monstrous beings, and if Sephia was going to make it out of this ordeal alive—and protect Nora in the process—then she would have to be *more* ruthless. More monstrous.

Prince Tarron could not kill anyone if Sephia killed him first.

And meanwhile, Nora could stay disguised and safe in Middlemage. She would feign an acute illness to explain away the sudden weakness and shaking, they'd decided. It was not so strange for a girl who had just lost her sister—her best friend—to take seriously ill, was it?

Their parents would be easy to fool; the king and queen were so caught up in outside affairs as of late that they likely wouldn't have noticed if Nora tap-danced naked through the cold marble halls of the Central Palace. A newly-acquired tremor would be overlooked, surely. Nana Rosa would be more difficult to deal with, but even she could be tricked for a few weeks, the sisters hoped.

One month.

This was the timeline Sephia had decided on for this mission.

Longer than that, and suspicions might begin to arise. Or the witch's spell might begin to weaken, or it might become irreversible; one could never tell with witch magic. And then, of course, there was Sephia's *own* magic to worry about...

But she could contain her magic for one month. She could last in *all* ways for one month. And that would be long enough to get the sham of a marriage over with, for her to get her bearings within the Sun Court, and for her to decide on a more detailed plan and carry it out. She could do this.

She *would* do this.

The horses trotted briskly through the woods. The

sisters didn't speak again until the sounds of a distant procession floated through the leaves, causing a visible shiver of apprehension to roll through Nora and her mount.

Sephia felt that same apprehension, but she refused to let it distract her from their plan. She cleared her throat and said: "There's a second vial of potion in that bag I gave you. Every seven days, take one-eighth of it. Add a drop of my blood to it first. You secured that vial somewhere safe, didn't you?"

Nora nodded, numbly.

"The witch said old blood would do well enough if you were only restrengthening an existing spell. You just can't let the spell wear off completely. Understand?"

Another nod.

Sephia pressed a hand to her heart, close to where she had tucked her own vials of potion and blood. She would have to find a way to slip them discreetly into her luggage before she left the kingdom. The dress she wore might have been pleasing to a fae prince, but it was not especially practical; it had infuriatingly few places in which to stash knives or vials of blood.

She gritted her teeth and nudged her horse into a faster trot, weaving recklessly through the trees, as if trying to shake off that apprehension that kept creeping after her.

Nora caught up with her easily—she had always been the better rider—and she said, "You know what they say about the prince, about his magic and his temper and his—"

"I know what they say."

"Are you sure you can...well, *you know*."

"Kill him?"

Nora winced.

Sephia smiled gently. "A bit late to be doubting me and our plan now, isn't it?"

"I..."

Sephia set her eyes back on the path before her, unwilling to entertain that doubt.

In one month, one way or another, Prince Tarron would be dead.

She would make it look like an accident.

It was custom in Middlemage for a widowed bride to not remarry, and Sephia intended to use this to her advantage. Once Prince Tarron was dead, she would plead with the Sun Court until they allowed her to go home and *mourn* with her family by herself. And surely they would agree; what use would they have for a weeping, devastated human amongst their bright and beautiful halls? She intended to appear annoyingly inconsolable—and she was a good actress.

She would have to be, to get those monstrous creatures to take pity on her and send her home.

But she *would* get them to do it.

She would come home, and then she and her sister could exchange places once more. Sephia would refocus on the throne she was set to inherit, and Nora would live out her life in peace, pretending to mourn the fae prince she had never truly had to marry.

Simple as that.

"I don't doubt you, Seph," said Nora, quietly. "I'm just afraid for you."

Sephia opened her mouth, intending to give a soothing response, but...

Was there a way to soothe her sister, considering the frightening precipice they were approaching?

She couldn't think of one, so she just kept riding.

CHAPTER 2

*T*hey made good time.

They turned only a few heads as their horse's hooves clopped against the stone of the sacred pavillion—and only human heads, at that; there were no fae to be seen yet, which meant that Sephia and Nora were not catastrophically late.

But now the hum of Sephia's anxious thoughts gained new lyrics: *Too soon, too soon, too soon...*

All too soon, they had reached this edge of their old life: the so-called *Unbreakable Bridge* stretched off to their right, ominous and golden and waiting. It had been built as a symbol of that ancient bargain between the human and fae— and the everlasting connection that bargain had forged. There was a second, identical bridge on the western side of the kingdom, stretching from Middlemage into *Nocturne*, the Shadow fae lands.

Forty-five years ago, the woman who would have been Sephia's aunt was taken across that second bridge and into Nocturne, never to return.

Today, the Court of the Sun would emerge to take their own bride across *this* bridge and back with them to Solturne.

The original bargain had been the idea of one of Middlemage's ancient kings. It had put an end to the constant warring between these two fae realms and turned Middlemage into a buffer, a neutral territory that neither the Sun nor Shadow courts had rights to cross. That king who put forth this treaty had twin daughters, and he had promised one to each of the fae courts as a show of faith and balance.

Some said that the fae had tricked that king into giving more than he'd meant to— that no future daughters of his bloodline had truly been offered in this bargain. The details of the event were shrouded in mystery, and they varied depending on who was telling the story.

But however it happened, here they were, approaching the tenth ceremonial taking of a Caster daughter.

There were paintings depicting this 'Taking' scattered throughout the Central Palace in Ocalith. Most were bright and airy, depicting a shining sacrifice and movements of magic that resulted in benevolent feelings between all of the involved parties.

But there were other, older paintings hidden away that were...*darker*.

Sephia had stumbled upon a stack of these other paintings once. Well, not so much *stumbled upon* as discovered them when she snuck into one of the library's off-limits storage rooms, much to the dismay of the old records-keeper. These earlier works were far more grue-some, depicting human brides with ripped dresses and crooked crowns stained with blood.

Ten years had passed since her discovery, but Sephia still remembered a particularly striking image of a young, bloodied princess sitting astride a great black horse. Her head had been high, and the look in her eyes had been piercing, defiant in spite of her shackles, even as she was being led away by two fae warriors.

Sephia did not know what to expect from the fae thieves coming today, but she knew there would be no blood spilled during this stealing. She would go quietly, as her kingdom expected Nora to.

And soon she would kill her target just as quietly.

No need for dramatics.

Along the banks of the river were shrines that were meant for offerings to the fae. They were all full. Almost every family in the capital city had a personal shrine, and in it they left the finest of whatever items they were best known for; there were priceless garments, various jewel-studded weapons, and food... *so much food.* The cloying scent of rotten fruit and the tang of spoiled vegetables mingled with the river's fishy smell.

Sephia's nose wrinkled, partly from the smell, and partly from an inward disgust toward it all.

The fae never touched any of the gifts left for them.

But if those gifts stopped being given, strange things always seemed to follow soon after. Crops failed. Chil-dren ran away and didn't return. The usually plentiful deer and other game in the forest thinned.

These things may have been coincidences, but the

people of Middlemage had long been convinced that they were punishments—and so the gifts were a necessary ward against those corrupt and easily-offended creatures they called *neighbors*.

People were checking the shrines and leaving fresh gifts even now. Several dozen of what appeared to be common townsfolk had accompanied the royal procession; likely they'd used the excuse of needing to tend to their respective shrines—though everyone present knew that they only wanted a chance to glimpse the fae.

What was it about monsters that enticed people to look? Sephia wondered.

This was the 'safest' opportunity to see them, she supposed—when they would be relatively caged by the bars of tradition and circumstance.

But if she'd had a choice, *she* wouldn't have been anywhere near this place.

She felt someone staring at her. She was unsurprised when she glanced to her left and saw Nana Rosa striding toward them.

The old woman's forehead glistened with *amalith* powder, as did the foreheads of many others around them. Only those with royal blood could see the fae unaided—another component of that ancient bargain. Others had to resort to wiping crushed amalith petals across their skin and putting drops of blessed water in their eyes. The combination of these two things made even the toughest person's eyes water, so their guardian's normally harsh gaze was tempered by tears, at least.

"What in the name of the three great gods have you

two been up to this morning?" demanded Nana Rosa in a fierce whisper.

"We were—"

"The queen was *beside* herself with concern, and the king has already required smelling salts *twice* today. They sent a small army's worth of soldiers into the woods to search for you—and for what? Only for you both to come traipsing in here as if nothing happened. *Honestly!*"

"We were close by," Nora insisted—in Sephia's body and through Sephia's voice. She gave no reason to suspect anything, and yet the real Sephia still tensed, wondering if their caretaker would notice that something was amiss.

But Nana Rosa only narrowed her gaze on the one she *thought* was Sephia, as she so often had in the past, and she snapped out another reprimand: "You should have been *here*, obediently waiting for your sister's ceremony. I know this disappearing act was your idea, Sephia; how many times have I told you not to drag your poor sister into your foolish games?"

"We didn't mean to be late."

"You've only known this day was coming for *your entire lives*, so why wouldn't—"

"We may never see each other again!" The words were in Nora's voice, but with the bite that usually accompanied Sephia's. "So maybe we lost track of our last moments together."

Nana Rosa turned slowly to face the one who looked like Nora, obviously shocked by that bite.

"We're here now," Sephia added, swallowing down her anger and trying to sound more like the peacemaker that the second-born twin usually was.

Nana Rosa studied her for a long, uncomfortable moment.

Then the old woman sighed her familiar, world-weary sigh. She still didn't appear suspicious; the uncharacteristic vitriol in this *Nora*'s tone could be explained away by nerves, after all. "Yes," she finally said. "I suppose you *are* here, aren't you?" She pursed her lips, and without another word, she led them to the party of royals that had gathered close to the bridge.

As they folded in amongst this party, Sephia and her twin were swiftly reprimanded by their parents. Sephia managed to slip away just long enough to tuck the witch's potion into one of her trunks—*Nora's* trunks, rather—alongside the vial of her sister's blood. But there was no time to bury these things too deeply.

A warm, violent breeze swept to life, scattering leaves across the surface of the river. A sudden hush settled over the crowd, and Sephia steadied herself and looked across the bridge.

There was nothing interesting to see.

Not at first.

But the in-sync clopping of two sets of hooves soon penetrated the silence, and then Sephia's chest tightened as two of the most beautiful horses she'd ever seen trotted over a hill on the other side of the river. Their manes were spun gold, their white flanks sparkling, their movements more like gliding than trotting.

They didn't look *real*.

But those horses were nothing compared to the beings riding them.

Before today, Sephia had only glimpsed the fae a

24

handful of times. She had locked eyes with one as a child, when a game of hide-and-seek had driven her carelessly deep into the woods. Another one had spoken to her from across the very river she stood before now, his voice honey-swirled and soft as a lullaby as he asked her what she was placing in the shrine at the water's edge. But everything else had been paintings and illustrations in books, which did no justice to the ones approaching them now.

Sephia stepped toward them as if pulled by an invisible rope.

The warm breeze that had heralded their approach seemed to be under their command. It swirled the leaves and bent the flowered tree branches away from them, creating a more clear path to walk along. Their hair was the same white-gold as their horses. The light armor they wore made no sound as they dismounted with slow, elegant motions.

Sephia watched them drop to the ground. If they had wanted to keep floating in the air, unhindered by something so silly as *gravity*, then she suspected they very well could have.

The hush over the crowd remained. Everyone had stopped moving. Everyone was mesmerized—including Sephia, though she had steeled herself against this very moment, knowing she needed to be fully aware during it. But they had stolen away that awareness so quickly and completely...

Was it magic at work?

Or worse, what if it *wasn't* magic?

If just the common soldiers were this beautiful and

mesmerizing without even trying, then what would the prince himself look like? It was hard not to wonder about it.

It doesn't matter how beautiful or mesmerizing he is, Sephia reminded herself.

All that mattered was that beautiful things could die just as easily as ugly things—as long as she herself stayed *focused*.

Nana Rosa's hand was on her shoulder, suddenly. Sephia was surprised by the gentle weight of it, the way it squeezed and seemed to be trying to offer stability. But this was hard on the old woman, wasn't it? She had been close to Nora, and that was who she *thought* she was saying goodbye to.

The king and queen, by comparison, appeared nothing but resigned—and this was *not* a surprise. They had been preparing for this moment since before their twins had been born. In eighteen years, they had not *once* let their children forget about the duty and destiny that awaited them.

This is the way of things.

How many times had their mother repeated that phrase?

Sephia had often wondered if her mother actually wanted children at all, or if she had been forced into it because of a sense of that duty and the need to hold up Middlemage's side of the bargain. She had not been cruel to Sephia or her sister during their eighteen years; just distant. Passive. And the king had been much the same.

The same villagers who made up lies about the princesses also liked to spout lies about how much those princesses hated their parents. The more dysfunctional the royal family seemed, the better the villagers felt about themselves, Sephia guessed. But the truth was that she did not hate the queen *or* the king.

She *nothinged* them.

Although sometimes that empty feeling ached worse than outright hatred.

A strange part of her was happy to be leaving that emptiness behind, if only for the next month. The happiness was fleeting, however; it vanished the instant a gilded carriage—one drawn by more of those unreal horses—rolled into sight.

The soldiers that had proceeded it each dropped to one knee. Most of the humans on the Middlemage side of the river followed suit. The king and queen did not kneel, but they bowed their heads. After a sharp nudge from Nana Rosa, Sephia did the same.

Sephia heard someone emerging from that gilded carriage—the fae king, someone announced. She desperately wanted to see him for herself. She still did not lift her head; Nora would have been more obedient. She had to remember that she was Nora now.

But she couldn't help but chance a glimpse from underneath her lashes.

The Sun King was radiant even in her peripheral vision. His clothes were glaringly white and embellished with shimmering gold thread. The many twisted prongs of his crown each caught a piece of the sun, occasionally blinding people when he tilted his head just so. He was talking in a low voice, the smooth words sounding more like a melody, like part of a song harmonizing with the river's current, than a proper speech.

Moments passed. A second being emerged from behind the king. *The prince*, Sephia heard someone whisper.

She could no longer keep her head lowered.

It lifted as if Prince Tarron had cupped a hand beneath her chin and lifted it himself. And she found him staring at her as though no space existed between them. As if no one else was standing within that circle of trees. The *intensity* of the gaze was undeniable, but she couldn't clearly make out the finer parts of his expression from across the river.

Though if she'd had to guess, she would have said those finer parts likely signaled intense *disgust*.

She felt compelled to stare back. She managed to hide her own disgust. Somehow. His appearance helped matters, she had to admit; it was...*difficult* to be entirely disgusted with the being she was staring at. Even from a distance, his otherworldly beauty was obvious enough.

He followed the king as that king stepped toward the bridge. Sephia followed her parents as they did the same. Both parties stopped on their respective sides, and said their respective, rehearsed pieces, and Sephia only partially listened to the ritualistic words. She had memorized them a long time ago, reciting the words to herself over and over when the nightmarish images of her future —the same images that were now playing out before her —kept her from sleeping.

She held her breath as she subtly studied more of the prince's appearance.

This was her target.

After years of planning, and those countless sleepless nights spent anticipating this moment...here it was.

Here *he* was.

And those golden horses looked like plain, common beasts, suddenly. Every creature—including the Sun King —looked plain and common compared to the prince.

Tarron's hair was not the pale, washed-out gold of bright sunlight like the king's and his soldiers; it was golden, but it made her think instead of a sunset with strands of red woven through it. The entirety of him suggested that dreamy, hazy space between day and night. Hooded eyes; a smile that held a memory of warmth but that chilled her the longer she stood there; a beauty that she found herself bracing against, because somehow it hinted at oncoming darkness.

His eyes seemed to sparkle a little more brightly with every downcast face they roved over. Was he enjoying the sight of people kneeling, cowering before him from a mixture of fear and awe?

Sephia's fists clenched at the thought. But then her parents dropped into a bow, and she found herself with no choice but to do the same.

They rose to the sight of the fae king beckoning the prince to his side.

It should have been that king striding forward to meet the rulers of Middlemage; that was the way of things. But to Sephia's surprise, the prince himself stepped forward —alone— to claim his own bride. The fae king braced a hand against one of the bridge's golden supports, and he simply watched.

Sephia's heart pounded a little more fiercely with every step the prince took toward her. Fear was finding cracks in her armor, seeping in despite all the time she had spent fortifying that armor.

Her mother's boney fingers were suddenly upon her back, caressing in a rough circle before giving a little pinch that made Sephia stiffen and draw her shoulders back. She didn't have to glance up at her mother's face to picture the stern expression upon it, and she could hear the unspoken command—

Stand up straight to greet your prince.

And so Sephia did.

Her eyes met his once more. She did not cower. She did not flinch as her mother and father stepped back, and she did not look away from the prince even as he took a golden bracelet from the pocket of his fine coat and motioned for her to give him her hand. Her twin had always had a quiet, stoic bravery about her, and Sephia found herself determined to mimic that bravery now.

The prince did not touch her as he clicked the bracelet into place. For something that looked so delicate, that bracelet felt surprisingly tight and heavy.

Not unlike a shackle.

"Are there any last words you would like to speak over your kingdom and its people?" he asked.

She was surprised by the question—it seemed almost like a polite gesture, and spoken in the tongue of her own kingdom, no less— but she thought it safer not to accept the offer.

Whenever possible, it was *always* safer not to accept whatever the fae offered.

"There is no need." Her eyes drifted toward the royal carriage adorned with her kingdom's flags. "We can just collect my things and go."

"Things?"

"Yes. My luggage."

"Luggage?" The word rolled off the prince's tongue as though it tasted so foul he'd considered spitting it out.

Sephia's cheeks burned in the heat of his suddenly furious gaze.

"Were you under the impression that you would not be well provided for once you returned to my palace?" His glare jumped to Sephia's parents.

The king visibly recoiled.

The queen managed a reply: "The girl has a mind of her own, I'm afraid. She insisted—"

"I see." Prince Tarron held up a hand. His long, elegant fingers curled into a fist as he continued: "And did you inform her that this mind of hers, along with every other part of her, now belongs to *me*?"

The queen opened her mouth to speak, but nothing came out.

Sephia glared at the prince until he canted his head back toward her. His eyes were an arresting shade of dark green, she noticed—like the moss that grew deep in the damp and fog-wrapped parts of the forest.

Beautiful.

Of course they were.

She briefly considered taking the pin from her hair and impaling one of those beautiful eyes with it, but she refrained.

No need for dramatics, she reminded herself.

"Yes, of course," said the queen, drawing the prince's gaze back to her. "We apologize. Leanora has every intention of fulfilling her duties as your bride, of course."

Leanora.

Nora would have nodded along with their mother's words, eager to please her.

Sephia *had* to go along with the queen, or else she risked failing her mission before it had even truly started. And yet she also had to find a way to take at least *some* of her luggage with her...

"There are things in those trunks that you cannot replace," she said, her tone as meek and pleading as she could make it.

The prince snorted. "Those *things* are no longer of any concern to you. You don't need them where you're going." His voice turned droll. "Think of it as an exciting chance to start a new life, completely unhindered by all of the garbage you collected in your old one. Not many people are gifted such things."

Sephia's disgust was dangerously close to sparking into something more violent.

How was she going to stomach being in close proximity with this beast for more than a few minutes? If this mission took an entire month...

Gods, I might be in trouble.

Thinking quickly, she swallowed her revulsion and spoke in a firm but polite voice: "Then at least permit me to say goodbye to one of those parts of my old life. And to take at least one of my family heirlooms with me; not so much a *need*, as I certainly don't expect that I will need anything other than you, my prince."

Silence.

"It is a *want*, not a need," she pressed. "If that makes any difference."

Every human present seemed to be leaning closer, astounded by her audacity and eager for the prince's undoubtedly vicious reply, but Sephia paid them no mind.

She didn't take her eyes off of Tarron. She was waiting —*hoping*, like a fool—that the cruel gleam in his eyes might soften into something kinder.

It didn't.

But soon that harsh gleam turned almost...*curious*.

And this was a dangerous look on his face for a myriad of reasons, not least of all because it somehow made him all the more attractive.

He turned away with another scoff. Sephia's heart began to sink, until she heard him mutter: "Very well. Be quick about it."

Sephia was quick indeed, and Nora was quicker; the younger twin was already at work, pawing through the trunk where Sephia had left those priceless vials. She turned and met Sephia as she approached, clutching a worn leather journal. The pages of this journal did not contain *written* secrets anymore; years ago, Sephia had hollowed out those pages and made a hole in which to nest treasures she wanted to keep hidden.

She didn't open the journal to check for anything now; she already knew what Nora had hidden inside it.

Nora's whisper was hoarse with grief and barely audible even as they stood close enough to press their foreheads together: "Promise me you'll come back."

Sephia swallowed hard. Her fingers fumbled between them, tightening the buckle that kept the journal closed.

Nora took her hand and squeezed it. "Come back to me," she whispered again.

Sephia squeezed back. "I love you, Nora."

The warm breeze swirled once more. The river slapped and sloshed against its banks, and Sephia looked back to the bridge, where the golden prince stood waiting. For her. Her breath nearly stopped at the sight. She squeezed her sister's hand more tightly, until she felt Nora's pulse throb against her own.

Nora's life.

That was why she was doing this.

That was why *she could do this.*

"I love you," she said, letting go, "and I will not fail you."

CHAPTER 3

"*I* detest the smell of humans," said the Sun King.

"Yes. So I've heard." Tarron offered his older brother a stardew apple from the basket tucked into the carriage's storage compartment; the fruit's powerfully tart fragrance was enough to drive away the memory of most other scents. "I believe you've mentioned it, oh, around thirty times this afternoon?"

King Deven accepted the fruit and then leaned back, stretched his long legs out in front of him. He winced a bit with the simple motion, but quickly covered his pain up with a lazy smile. "Just making conversation."

The prince acquiesced with a mere shrug, though he silently agreed; humans all smelled like forged metal and gunpowder to him. Like *unnatural* things.

His bride-to-be had been no exception— though there had also been another scent clinging to her that he couldn't place, something that had struck him as neither particularly natural *or* unnatural. Something that made him uneasy.

But then again, *most* of what had taken place at that bridge had made him uneasy.

They were at least twenty miles from that human kingdom now—already well past the Veil that separated their realms— and he was only just starting to breathe normally again, and to relax the tension from his muscles.

Their carriage bumped along. The brothers were silent for several miles, until Deven, who was never content with silence for long, cleared his throat and said, "Ah, but we're almost back to the Solturne border—and better smells— thankfully." He looked to Tarron, clearly expecting his younger brother to offer his opinion on the matter.

"Yes," Tarron said. "So we are."

Tarron's gaze shifted to one of the windows of their carriage, to the slashes of countryside that were visible through swaying curtains.

They were rolling over the Bloodroot Fields, and the hazy outlines of the distant, hillside houses of Solturne's Outer Ring were starting to take shape. When they were younger— and both of them carefree and overconfident princes— they used to make a game of trying to catch and ride the wild elk that roamed these poppy-strewn fields. A dangerous sport, but certainly not the *most* dangerous game they had played growing up.

Those games had all stopped nearly a decade ago now, soon after the fateful night when the walls of the royal city had been overtaken by the *belegor*. Those shadowy, shapeshifting beasts had been swiftly driven out, but not before one of them found its way into the chambers of the sleeping king and queen.

It had taken three days and a small army's worth of servants to clean all of the blood from the walls and furniture.

The death of their parents had thrust Deven onto the throne long before he was prepared to take it, and there he remained.

So they couldn't afford to play any other dangerous games now.

Not when they were already tied up in the ever more dangerous games of politics and crowns, of treaties and bargains...

"So it's done, then." Deven paused. Waited again for Tarron to offer his own commentary. When the prince remained silent, the king sighed. "Well? What do you think of your bride-to-be?"

"What should I be thinking, precisely?"

Deven huffed at the question. "What should you be thinking? What a ridiculous question! Think your own thoughts, my dear little brother."

Tarron arched a brow. "Our subjects expect me to feel a certain way about the matter; you know this as well as I do. The marriage fulfills our side of the bargain. It continues Middlemage's obligation as a buffer between our lands and Nocturne, and it will unlock my magic... these are the important things, and they are the only things that I am *thinking* about."

"Yes, but how do you *feel* about her?"

"I don't intend to mix my precious feelings with my

duties, thank you kindly." He absently rolled the sleeves of his shirt up and touched the golden bracelet that was resting, smooth and cold, against his skin. It matched the one he'd wrapped around the princess's wrist. "They're irrelevant to most of our subjects, and therefore they're irrelevant to me."

"You should care less about what those subjects expect of you."

"And you should care more."

"Perhaps I will, one day," said the king with a roguish grin. But they both knew he wouldn't. Deven had never cared what his subjects thought of him. "But then again, I suspect my reputation is too far gone to save, so why bother?" he added with a quiet laugh.

The corner of Tarron's mouth twitched as he fought off a frown. He cared deeply for his older brother, but sometimes...

Sometimes, he felt as if Deven had inherited the crown from their father, but that he himself had taken on its weight. And he also cared deeply about the lands that crown oversaw, which made his brother's casual attitude all the more difficult to deal with.

His eyes fell on Deven's hands. One of them had started to shake. The king subtly attempted to slide it into the pocket of his coat, but he moved too slowly; Tarron had already gotten a good look at it.

It was yet another part of their lives that was growing more dangerous by the day.

"Your illusion spell has faded," Tarron said. The skin on his brother's hand was terribly dark—almost black, rather than the pale grey color it had been for the past several months. "And how long has it looked that awful? It's getting worse, I think."

"It's been a long day. I didn't even think of it." Deven waved the concern away with his unpocketed hand, as though it was an annoying fly that had slipped into their carriage. He clearly wanted Tarron to drop the subject.

"That young woman...my *bride*," the prince continued anyways, "it's true what we'd heard of her appearance; she *does* have a grayish tint to her skin, not unlike what the skin of your own hand looked like just a few weeks ago."

Deven said nothing.

"Which lends credence to what some of our scholars have been saying, doesn't it? That this curse— or sickness, or spell, or whatever it might be—effects those with a strong affinity for the Sun. Princess Leanora should have a fair amount of the old goddess's power within her, thanks to the bargain. Her ailment could very well be related to yours."

All fae were descendants of the gods and goddesses that had once roamed across their world, and many carried these *affinities* for magic because of this—whether it was for Sun, or Shadow, or Fire or Ice or any of the countless others. The ones with the most magic had leveraged their power into crowns and kingdoms a long time ago, and Tarron's ancestors were among the earliest and most powerful of those crowned ones.

His brother was no exception to their powerful bloodline. The king's magic had the potential to blind and scorch entire armies—but more often, Deven had used it for good, aiding the growth of crops and otherwise providing light and life to this part of the world they ruled over.

And Tarron himself would have been able to do the same sort of things, *if* he had been born first.

But because of that strange, long-ago bargain with the human kingdom, part of Tarron's magic was bound elsewhere. Namely, his bride-to-be had the other part—at least until the marriage and its associated rituals took place and unlocked it.

So this arranged marriage would be useful for *something*, at least.

"I've spoken at length with the Middlemage king, and he assures me that the girl has certain quirks, yes —like the odd pallor of her skin," said Deven. "She *also* doesn't seem to have much natural skill with magic, he admits. But otherwise she is perfectly healthy."

Tarron was unconvinced. "You know, there are some who believe that Princess Leanora's sickness is a result of the other twin—the Shadow twin's—magic. Which is interesting, given what happened the night *your* illness first appeared."

Deven's ever-present grin was beginning to wilt in the corners. "Can we just celebrate your upcoming nuptials and forget about these dark matters for a day?"

"It's worth investigating more closely, is all I'm suggesting."

"As I told you, the Middlemage king has said—"

"Who cares what he's said? He could be lying."

"He wouldn't risk such an offense. He's too much of a fat coward for that."

"Well perhaps he *hopes* he's telling the truth," said Tarron, "but hope alone does not make a thing true."

The king chuckled, shaking his head. "Gods, you've become entirely too serious in your old age."

"I'm twenty-seven." Hardly old, especially for their kind, who occasionally lived to be well over two-hundred.

"Are you?" Deven pretended to look shocked. "The First Goddess as my witness, I would have sworn you were at *least* three times that age, based on the amount of grumbling and worrying you do."

One of us has to worry, Tarron wanted to say.

Instead, he pulled the sleeves of his shirt back down, covering up that heavy golden bracelet, and he calmly stated: "If the sickness progresses, and it takes you—"

"I'm not dying anytime soon, little brother. Put the thought out of your mind. Let those scholars and advisors of ours worry about curses and spells. You should be focused on your new bride." His grin suddenly returned in full earnest. "She did not seem especially... *taken* with you at the riverside, did she?"

Tarron sighed.

Deven took a bite of his apple, still grinning, and then he continued—spewing little flecks of fruit flesh as he spoke: "You pulled off the arrogant, beastly persona quite well; the humans all looked properly terrified of you. Father would have been proud."

"Yes, well, the humans have been drifting too close to our borders these past years. They needed a reminder that we can be *beastly* so that they'll stay away. It's for the good of both of our worlds that we don't mix anymore than we have to."

"Somehow I don't think your princess will see your behavior as entirely altruistic." Deven finished his snack and carelessly tossed the core back into the basket with the uneaten fruit, which made Tarron cringe. "So worry about *her*, if you want to worry about something," he pressed, focused entirely on changing the subject now.

Of course he was.

Tarron leaned his head against the carriage wall and held in another sigh. Conversations about his brother's strange illness never took long to veer off in different directions.

"Put my problems out of your mind," Deven repeated, his tone bordering on serious for once.

The prince went back to watching the world outside. They were leaving the fields behind, winding their way around the base of the Mount Amaros, and the carriage holding the princess rolled briefly into sight before disappearing around a tight bend on the path ahead.

He felt a strange tug in his chest— brief but powerful, almost painful— as she disappeared from view.

It was tradition for her to ride separately, as any stolen *prisoner* should. But for a moment, he wished he had insisted on doing away with that particular tradition— though it could have been worse; his ancestors had been far more barbaric about the matter. Princess Leanora was riding in her own separate carriage, yes, but a century ago that carriage would have had bars and shackles instead of plush cushions and velvet curtains.

Still, a cage was a cage, wasn't it?

And it would have been nice to speak with her in private before they arrived at Solturne Hall. Not because he wanted to get to know her, but because he wanted to make sure she understood the rules of this game they were playing. He had enough to worry about without a difficult human girl making a mess of things.

Perhaps he could arrange a moment alone before all the dinners and parties and their other binding ceremonies got underway...

"Tarron?"

"Hm?"

"Still scheming to yourself, aren't you?"

"I was just enjoying the scenery."

Deven hesitated, and then he said, "You know, if I could change things, I would."

"Change things?"

"If this marriage wasn't so...*necessary*, I mean."

"It's fine."

Deven looked unconvinced.

"Really," Tarron insisted. "I don't need true love or happily-ever-afters or anything of the sort. I'm not...well, *you*."

Deven laughed. "And that's probably for the better, really. Imagine if we were both annoying, sappy fools— what a *disaster* that would be, eh?"

"I didn't say that."

"No," the king mused, "but I can easily imagine our subjects saying precisely those words."

"Don't be ridiculous."

Deven sighed a good-natured sigh, ran his fingers through his hair, and then settled back into his seat and closed his eyes.

Tarron watched him for a moment, until— just as it

always did— any ire that he'd felt melted away. This was his brother, for better or worse, after all. The only family he had left.

"Anyway, I believe someone once told me..." Tarron began, his tone lighter "...that you should care less about what those subjects expect of you."

Deven smiled without opening his eyes.

Tarron returned that smile this time, but he was glad that his brother wasn't actually looking at him—because he doubted the expression came across as genuine.

He couldn't remember the last genuine laugh or smile he'd had; they were few and far between since his brother's ascension.

Deven's rule had been unexpected, and a jarring departure from the king that had preceded him. Their father had ruled without fear or mercy, and their subjects had loved him for it.

But Deven was softer.

Weaker.

Some claimed that it was that weakness that had led to him getting sick, and to the other problems they'd been facing in recent years—such as the humans creeping ever closer to their sacred lands.

And now those subjects were uneasy at best. They were already planning for what came *after* Deven's death. *He isn't strong enough to last*, they said. The silver lining to losing their king, whispered the same voices, was that Prince Tarron would take his place. *And perhaps this boy will be more like his father.*

But Tarron didn't have any desire to become king— especially at the cost of losing his brother. He only wanted the stable, peaceful life he had once known. Which was why he had insisted on carrying through with the tradition of marrying the Middlemage princess.

This marriage is a step towards stability, he kept telling himself.

Once he had his bride, he would have his full magic. He would have better connections to the Middlemage court, too, and to their army that had proven themselves useful allies in the past.

They had lost so much over the years... he was not prepared to lose anything else. He would do what he had to do, even if it meant putting aside his personal feelings and carrying through with this ridiculous marriage business.

He just hoped his bride-to-be proved cooperative.

CHAPTER 4

*S*ephia was trying her best to be cooperative.

But the servants of Solturne Hall were making it *difficult*.

Over the past hours she had been poked. Prodded. Pulled at. Fussed at. Dressed and undressed, styled and restyled. She had been mocked as well, she was fairly certain; the fae women tending to and torturing her spoke the common tongue of Middlemage well enough, but they seemed to prefer speaking in their own language. And though Sephia had studied what she could of that language in preparation for her time here, there were intricacies and intonations that were simply impossible for human ears—for *her* ears—to grasp.

Nevertheless, she endured the ordeal without protest, just as Nora would have.

When it was finished, her hair was piled into intricate braids woven through with chains of white flowers, and she wore a white dress that dipped elegantly low against her back. The dress's draping material was thin, and she couldn't suppress the shivers that erupted across her bare arms as the servants stepped away to study their creation from a distance.

Those servants finally nodded their begrudging approval. They fell back into their secretive, possibly mocking, chatter, and Sephia picked up her skirts and moved toward the window— toward the sunlight shining in—hoping for warmth.

Her room had a view, at least.

Far below, the flowering courtyards of Solturne Hall crisscrossed in alternating rows of brilliant color. The wind swirled pink and white petals through the air in a mesmerizing dance that was set to the tune of nobles laughing and birds singing. Even through the glass, the song filled Sephia with an ache that was not altogether unpleasant. She pressed her forehead against the window, and her eyes briefly fluttered shut as she soaked in the warmth and the sounds.

When her eyes opened again, the first thing they fell upon was a tall tower of white brick, adjacent to her own. It had no windows. Storage, or perhaps a library of some sort? Or some other secret place they were protecting from sunlight, or from outside eyes for some reason...?

Her gaze dropped to the base of the tower, seeking its entrance. She wondered when—and *if*—she might be permitted to explore her new 'home' more thoroughly.

A shadow moved across the white brick.

It moved swiftly and strangely enough that it caught Sephia's attention and held it, and after a moment of staring she would have *sworn* she was watching it turn into something more solid. Something with a distin-

47

guishable head. With two legs. With swinging arms and clawed hands.

There were perhaps a dozen fae strolling the grounds below her, but none of them seemed to notice that anything was amiss.

Sephia pushed the window open—she was pleasantly surprised to find she wasn't *completely* locked in—and she leaned out and narrowed her sight toward that white tower, toward that shadowy beast—

Gone.

There were no shadows to see aside from the thin fingers of darkness cast by a few willow trees swaying in the breeze. Normal shadows…

That was *all* there had ever truly been, most likely.

Anything else was simply her imagination running wild. It must have been. She had read and heard so many terrible things about this place and its inhabitants that even the shadows seemed menacing. An odd thing for her, considering that she usually felt most at home when she was surrounded by shadows, thanks to that magic she had been born with.

She had been trying not to think about that magic.

But suddenly it was difficult *not* to think about it; she could feel the servants behind her, watching her.

They were staring at the *Sun* twin, as far as they knew.

She didn't intend to stay here long enough for them—or the prince— to discover that her magic was the opposite of what it should have been. If the Sun Prince or any of his servants suspected her of courting with shadows, the consequences would, of course, be deadly.

And she was not dying here.

Such deceit was possible only because she had been working to suppress her magic for her entire life. When she was younger, the shadows had often whispered to her. Other times, she had managed to control them into doing her bidding without really meaning to do it; they stole secrets from passersby, created distractions that helped her sneak into places she shouldn't have been. Once, her shadows had even taken a physical hold on one of the palace servants. Sephia had caught him harassing her sister, and she hadn't thought about what she was going to do, she just *did* it.

He swore she had possessed him. That he had heard her voice whispering in his mind, telling him what to do as the shadows she commanded wrapped more tightly around him.

The servant had been let go after that incident— though not before receiving a handsome amount of money in exchange for his promised discretion.

Sephia had been grounded for a month for her crime, even though she hadn't meant to use her magic on the man. And he had *deserved* it, either way.

Occasionally, she had longed to do more with her powers. But her parents and the rest of the Middlemage court had allowed her to study that magic only enough to keep it under control. Because what use did a future *human* queen have for such wild power? It was undignified, they said.

Now that she was older, she realized that calling it 'undignified' just meant they were afraid of it. She had shown more magic than any Shadow twin before her, and the only person who *didn't* fear her for this was Nora.

49

All the more reason why Sephia couldn't lose her.

Another flicker of darkness beckoned in the corner of her vision.

Was it really just the swaying trees?

It didn't matter; she turned away this time.

There was a knock at the door a moment later. One of the servants opened it to reveal the prince on the other side, and then that servant and all of the others placed a fist across their hearts and bent at the waist.

Sephia's skin suddenly felt too hot and too tight for her body.

But she did not bow.

She might have—it would have been the smarter, less suspicious thing to do—but she was too distracted by the prince's appearance at first.

He had changed as well. He no longer wore his traveling attire, but a much more regal-looking ensemble that included a fine silk shirt and a sparkling sapphire ring that hummed with what felt like powerful magical energy. A simple circlet sat upon his wavy hair, which was loosely fastened at the nape of his neck. Around his wrist, there was a golden bracelet identical to the one he'd forced onto her.

Had he been wearing it at the bridge?

He's shackled too, at least, she couldn't help but think.

He stepped closer to her in the same confident way he'd stepped across the Unbreakable Bridge: As if he commanded the space and everything in it.

He does, she reminded herself.

He wore a shackle, but he also carried the key. This was *her* room, she'd been told, but even it was connected to the prince's own room by way of a short hall. Because she was to be an extension of him.

She belonged to him, now, as he'd said.

She was a symbol, not unlike that crown upon his head. And that Sun magic that she didn't have...if she *had* had it, it would have been his to command as well. The stolen bride was a gift, a vessel of magic to be used and then discarded, nothing more.

She inwardly bristled at the thought, but she managed to keep her outward appearance passive. She did take a few steps away from the prince, but only went so far as the bedroom's sitting area. There was a beverage tray resting on the ottoman between the various chairs and the sofa; she perched on the edge of the pin-striped sofa and pretended to make herself a cup of tea.

She had no intentions of drinking it.

She didn't trust any of the food or drink in this place; the fae of both courts had a notorious reputation for playing amusing—and occasionally deadly—games with food and drink. One of their more unforgivable crimes to Sephia, as she was a tremendous fan of both cooking *and* eating.

There had been a month's worth of her own safe and specially-prepared food in her luggage because of this very reason.

Another complication of having to leave that luggage behind, she thought, bitterly.

But she would make do. Somehow. There had to be *something* safe to consume here—she just didn't think it wise to experiment with such things until she was alone. Knowing her luck, one sip of her tea would have her hallucinating, dancing on the table or trying to climb out the window while her fiancé gleefully watched.

As she stirred her tea, the servants shuffled off without a word, leaving her alone with that husband-to-be of hers.

Or she *thought* they were alone, at least—until an odd scratching came from the chair across from her. She placed her cup back on the tray and narrowed her eyes, searching.

Some sort of...*creature* was hooked over the top of that chair, peering back at her.

She thought it was a cat at first. It had the tufted ears of a feline, and slender, jewel-blue eyes that studied her with that particularly haughty, disdainful look that all cats seemed to be masters of. But then it toppled over and down onto the cushions, and she saw there was a beak where its snout should have been, and that it had... *wings.* They unfurled, and it righted itself with a few feathery flaps. Its long tail swept back and forth across the cushions, and it was tufted. Lion-like.

A griffin?

She had seen such creatures in books, but never one this small.

Regardless of its size, it had teeth sharp enough to tear flesh—and it bared them in her direction as it swooped closer.

Sephia swatted instinctively at the miniature beast, which snapped those razor teeth in response. Alarmed, she threw a worried glance at the prince.

But rather than alarmed, Prince Tarron looked... *amused.*

Sephia took a step away from the snapping beast. She attempted a brave, unbothered tone as she asked: "Are you familiar with this...this *creature?*"

"His name is Ketzal."

Ketzal growled. He lifted himself higher with a few tiny flaps, until he was eye-to-eye with Sephia.

"And are you...are you going to call him off before he bites me in the face?"

"Wouldn't do any good," drawled the prince as he walked over to the window and peered out. "He's notoriously bad at following commands. He's the only one in the palace that gets away with such disobedience."

The creature gave a little snort, as if proud of this fact.

Sephia lifted her hand, annoyed by the prince's indifference and thinking of swatting at the creature again. But she refrained. "Could you at least *try* to call him off?" she asked through clenched teeth.

"He only wants the pastries behind you," said the prince, still sounding amused. "He's a bit of a sugar fiend."

Sephia glanced over her shoulder, where indeed there was a second tray of refreshments resting on the table behind the sofa. It was piled high with colorful tarts and other sugar-dusted delicacies that she somehow hadn't noticed before.

She carefully stepped aside, her eyes locked with the griffin's.

He waited until she was completely out of his path. Then, with another throaty growl, he swooped past her and dove head first into the tray.

Several pastries went flying as he dug into them;

Sephia had to duck to avoid taking a cupcake to the face. A danish landed in her lap, and Ketzal followed an instant later, curling up on her new dress and proceeding to rip the fruit-filled treat to shreds.

"Messy thing, isn't he?"

"Mm." Tarron leaned against the wall, a hint of amusement still dancing in his eyes. The sunlight beaming in through the window seemed to follow his movements, as if he was subtly controlling it, making it highlight all of his best features.

The effect was dizzying to look at, so Sephia looked at the creature in her lap instead.

"But on the plus side," the prince continued, "like most creatures I've encountered, he's much friendlier once he has a full stomach."

Sephia picked up the fallen cupcake and offered it to the tiny griffin. He sniffed it cautiously for a moment before opening his jaws wide. In one bite, he inhaled the entire cloud of violet-colored frosting from its top. In the next bite, he'd finished off the rest—paper wrapper and all.

"And now he's willing to be your best friend, I imagine," said the prince.

The creature burped in response.

"Oh. Well, nice to meet you then, Ketzal." Soft laughter spilled from Sephia before she could stop it.

She felt the prince staring.

He quickly averted his eyes when she looked up, as though he hadn't meant for her to catch him.

"He belonged to my mother," he said after a long pause. "She found him half-drowned in the Eldon River.

Rescued him. His wings were broken—they still don't work very well. My father insisted we should put him out of his misery, but she refused. She was always doing things like that."

"She was fond of animals?"

The prince nodded. Stiffly. And then he went back to staring out the window.

Typical fae, she thought. *Incapable of a prolonged, civilized conversation.*

And yet his mother apparently had been capable of compassion toward small, wounded animals—which didn't seem to fit the beastly image of the fae that Sephia had built in her mind.

Strange.

Ketzal curled up amongst a pile of throw pillows, stretched out on his back, and promptly fell asleep with one paw resting across his bloated belly.

Sephia set about cleaning up his mess. She moved in a slow, distracted manner; her gaze kept drifting toward Tarron and focusing on him before she could help herself.

Finally, the prince spoke again, keeping his back to her as he asked: "Are you settling in?"

Here we go, she thought, and took a deep breath. *Now the real acting begins.*

She stood, brushing pastry crumbs from her dress; that dress didn't appear stained or torn, thankfully. "Well enough, my prince."

"Good."

She continued to fidget with the folds of her dress while she searched her mind for a safe topic. "The servants seemed to think that you would like this dress. And they insisted it was more suitable for the fine halls of my new home, as opposed to the one I was wearing before."

"And what do *you* think of it?"

Sephia was taken aback by the question.

I don't care for it. I want my old dress back. The one that smells like my real home. Like my sister—

Is that what he wanted her to say? Did he *want* her to challenge him? It seemed almost as if he was testing her, waiting for her retort. She hadn't bowed to him earlier. Had he noticed that?

She quickly decided that she couldn't risk appearing so rebellious, so early.

"If you like it, then so do I," she lied dutifully.

He stepped toward her.

She was suddenly, intimately aware of the thinness of her dress once more. Of the way his eyes lingered on the places where the fabric clung most completely.

"You're shivering," he commented.

She didn't reply.

"Are you cold?"

"A...a bit."

He moved closer. Circled her, his gaze still unapologetically drinking her in. "They tell me you don't have much skill with magic; but surely you at least have enough to warm yourself? You don't have to be afraid to use your magic here, you know."

"I know."

But she, of course, had no power to warm herself.

That was Sun magic, not Shadow magic. The potion she'd taken could not give her that.

Focus, she commanded herself. She needed a distraction, an excuse to give. One occurred to her almost immediately, and though she was loathe to use it, she didn't hesitate. She glanced up at him beneath fluttering eyelashes—in a way that she hoped passed for flirtatious—and she quietly said, "It isn't only the cold that is making me shiver, my prince."

He stopped moving. His eyes fixed on hers.

So bright.

So intense.

Staring into them made her feel a bit light-headed, and for an instant, her thoughts started down a treacherous path. She wondered what it might be like to look into those eyes every day. What it might feel like if his arm wrapped around her and pulled her closer. Steadied her. If his fingers brushed her cheek. If his magic warmed her. And she *did* shiver a little more at the thought, if only for that instant...

But then she steadied her own self—she didn't need *him* for that—and she said, "I simply meant...I've thought about this day for some time."

He blinked. Looked away again. Had he almost fallen into the same treacherous trance as her?

"It's a bit overwhelming to finally be experiencing it, I suppose," she added.

That wasn't entirely a lie.

He nodded. His expression was difficult to read, partly because he still wasn't truly looking at her.

"It all seems so much more...serious, now."

57

"Serious?" he repeated.

"Does it not please you that I am taking it as such, my prince?"

He casually rolled the sleeves of his shirt up to his elbows, one after the other, revealing a jagged scar on his left forearm. Sephia wondered if Ketzal was responsible for it. "It doesn't *please* me for you to call me *my prince*," he said.

She stiffened. "We aren't yet wed. I can't call you 'husband'."

"You could call me by my name."

"Is your false name so different from me calling you 'my prince'? At least the latter is true enough."

His lips parted and closed. Parted and closed. Speechless for the moment, because he clearly had no intention of revealing his true name to her. Not yet, anyway. Not that she'd expected him to—but it had been worth a try, hadn't it? True names held power. The sort of power that might come in handy in the weeks to come.

"Never mind my name," he finally said, a slight snarl slipping into the words. "And just so we're clear, I'm glad to see you're taking this seriously. You have a role to play in this palace, in this...*arrangement*, and I only came up here to make certain you were aware of what is expected of you. I can't have you causing trouble."

How romantic.

The words left a lingering sting, but why should they? She hadn't come here for romance. She had come here to slay a monster.

"Do I need to spell it out further for you, or do we have an understanding?"

What she wouldn't have given to be able to slay him *now*, and to simply end this charade.

But Sephia did not break character. She lowered her eyes—the perfect picture of *demure*—and she said, "We have an understanding."

"Good."

She lifted her gaze to find him smiling at her.

It wasn't a proper smile; she had yet to see him truly *smile*, she realized. Rather, it seemed he had a dozen different ways of lifting the corners of his mouth, of showing his sharp teeth, of trailing his tongue over his lips in ways that seemed inviting at first, but dangerous upon closer inspection.

Watching him now made Sephia think of the cautionary tales she'd heard about the Sun fae and the magic they used to lure unsuspecting humans into their world. They created circles of sunlight—bright and warm and inviting circles—but once a person stepped into that ring of light, they became blind. Defenseless.

Look twice before you step into the light, the Middlemage elders always used to say.

"You will dine with myself and my inner court tonight," Tarron informed her. "But before you can sit at our table, there are a few examinations that you need to undergo."

"Examinations?" The huff of protest escaped her before she could stop it. Hadn't she been poked and prodded enough today? And the word *examination* felt so cold. Disgusting. Barbaric.

What parts of her, precisely, did they feel the need to *examine*?

59

The prince clasped his hands behind his back, studying her again, looking entirely unsympathetic. And was it her imagination, or did he also seem a touch smug? As if he'd caught her in the middle of something heinous?

Sephia's blood chilled at this last thought.

Did they already suspect her trickery, somehow?

"Your father mentioned that you have some chronic health concerns. We have our own doctors here, and they need to be familiar with you and your...*conditions*. Or did you have a problem with us trying to help you?"

She shook her head; to do anything else in that moment would have been asking for trouble, and she already had enough trouble to sort through.

"That's what I thought." He stepped closer. Cupped her chin. Lifted her gaze to his. The warmth of his fingers and the ice of his eyes set off a multitude of conflicting feelings in her. "So you will not give Doctor Elric any problems. Is that understood?"

She offered a curt nod. It was enough to satisfy him, apparently, because he let her go and then headed for the door.

She watched him leave, her chest pounding. "*Monsters.*"

She didn't realize she'd said the word out loud until the prince paused with his hand on the doorknob. She thought she'd seen his pointed ears twitch, too, picking up that word that had been little more than a faint whisper as it escaped her.

He turned, and she fought the urge to shrink away from his gaze as he asked, "Did you say something?"

She shook her head. Then she finally made herself bow to him—only because doing so meant she didn't have to look into his piercing gaze.

He left without another word.

And this time, she waited until the door was closed behind him before she muttered, "I said nothing at all, *my prince*."

CHAPTER 5

The doctor arrived only minutes after Prince Tarron left.

"Doctor Elric," he told Sephia, and this was *all* he told her before he went to work, picking up where the servants had left off in their torturing. He used strange instruments to inspect her eyes, her ears, her throat. Most of them were sharp. All of them were cold. He studied her pulse and her breathing, took several vials of blood, and he muttered to himself all the while.

Sephia was a breath away from panicking the entire time.

He's going to realize I'm hidden by witch magic.

Any moment now, he's going to realize the truth, and perhaps he'll scream for the guards, or the king, or he'll kill me himself—

But he never did any of these things.

After what felt like an hour at least, he stopped poking and prodding and instead reached for one of the many medicinal jars he'd brought, this one filled to the brim with some sort of salve that smelled like ash with a hint of flowers. He dabbed his thumb into the salve, swirled it around, brought it up and swept it across the back of Sephia's neck.

A tingling started at the base of her skull and swept down her back. It felt like her skin was being peeled away. Like whatever magic he'd used was searching her for buried secrets. She thought again of her visit to the witch in the Ocalith Woods, and a shudder ripped through her.

"Keep still," Doctor Elric ordered.

Sephia kept still, but she could not keep silent. "What is that you're using? That stuff on your fingers?"

"An old diagnosing trick."

"And what are you hoping to *diagnose*?"

The doctor sighed, pushing a few strands of his long white hair behind his tapered ears. "I am simply making certain that you aren't carrying anything that could be dangerous to our kind. Your father himself warned us of a sickness that has long ailed you."

"I'm not contagious." Sephia gritted her teeth. She used to hate it when the Middlemage children teased Nora and acted as though getting too close to her would be the end of them. If whatever her little sister carried was contagious, Sephia would have caught it herself a long time ago.

The doctor grunted. "You never know with humans."

You never know with the fae, she wanted to snap in response.

She was going to end up losing her tongue at this rate, as often as she kept having to bite it.

63

The doctor said nothing else, just went back to shoving his cold instruments against her skin and muttering. He was callous, rough. He treated her like a prisoner instead of a princess—and like a prisoner sentenced to death, no less. Almost as if he suspected that she would be sentenced to such a fate before the day was over with.

Of course, he wasn't entirely *wrong* to suspect her. She was hiding things, after all.

But he didn't know that.

And when she breathed in deep and thought *rationally* about the matter, she was certain that she hadn't given anyone in this palace any real, outward reasons for them to be suspicious.

So by the time the doctor had finished, Sephia's entire body was burning with indignation— and with the feeling that her beliefs had been confirmed even further: There was no spare kindness here. Only cold, ever-suspicious monsters who wanted to treat humans like dirt.

The only creature who had showed her anything resembling warmth was Ketzal—and that was only because she'd offered him sweets, wasn't it?

That tiny creature finally woke from his nap amongst the pillows as the doctor left. He rolled off the sofa and nearly collided with the ground, but flared his wings at the last moment and managed to slow himself enough to land on his feet.

Sephia picked up one of the remaining desserts and held it out to him. "Can you track down Prince Tarron for me?" she asked.

Ketzal hesitated—perhaps it was the lingering touch

of indignant fire that had slipped into Sephia's voice—but in the end, the sugary goodness won the griffin over. He finished the offered treat in one gulp. Burped. Lifted into the air, flew several circles around Sephia's head, and then he shot towards the door.

THEY SPENT at least ten minutes attempting to find Tarron, but they were unsuccessful. By then, Sephia had cooled down enough to think clearly—which was probably for the best. If they *had* found him before this point, it likely would have resulted in disastrous consequences for her grander mission.

Sephia sighed. "Doesn't seem like he's anywhere around here."

Ketzal soared back to her and perched on her shoulder, his tufted tail twitching and his head tilting from side to side as he sniffed at the air. He seemed confused.

"You're messy and a bit useless," she mused, scratching the downy patch of fur on his chest. "But at least you're cute."

The griffin purred his agreement before settling more completely against her, draping himself like a dishrag over her shoulder.

He had led her outside. A labyrinth of hedges, trees, and vine-wrapped walls stretched before them, interspersed with occasional open spaces that featured elaborate statues and fountains.

The number of fae milling about seemed to have decreased since Sephia had peered down on this space from her room. Daylight was fading, and it was easy enough to find paths that were completely empty...and she found strolling along these courtyard paths infinitely preferable to staying in her room, or to strolling through the halls inside.

"Let's go exploring, shall we?" she asked Ketzal.

The griffin made an uncertain noise deep in his throat. But he clung tighter to her shoulder, and Sephia took this as a reluctant *yes*.

It was much warmer here than it had been in Middlemage, even with the wind that occasionally stirred into violent gusts. The air was thick with the scent of flowers, and every corner she turned seemed to lead to a new kind of these flowers. Rows of trees, heavy with foreign fruits, shaded parts of her walk, and she was grateful for the shadows that further concealed her. She felt as if she was slipping into a trance as she walked through it all.

Maybe I am.

At the very least, the growth of all of these flowers and fruits was likely aided by Sun magic. There was no telling how much of that magic lingered in the spaces around the plants, or how it might affect a human such as herself. Dread seized her at the thought.

She gave her head a little shake. The hazy, dreamlike feeling lingered. Ketzal purred softly, the sound vibrating against her skin. It was getting even warmer, and suddenly she didn't *want* to wake up.

But she didn't have a choice. Minutes later—or was it seconds? hours?—something shook her violently from her trance. A sound. One in her imagination, she thought, until there it was again: A grunt, and then a low, beastly cry that was cut short by a cough.

Ketzal lifted from her shoulder and darted for the garden's exit.

Sephia hesitated.

She should have followed the griffin.

But her curiosity quickly squashed her cautionary side —as it often did—and she crept in the direction of the noise.

She soon found herself at what appeared to be a dead-end. A stone wall at least several feet higher than herself stood before her. The sound had come from the other side of this wall. She was certain of this, somehow, even though she could not see what had caused that sound. She found a protruding brick in the wall, one sticking out just far enough for her to manage a foothold. She hoisted herself onto it, struggled to find balance, stood on her tiptoes, and peered over to see...

The king.

She quickly dropped back out of sight.

What was he doing out here alone?

And that noise a moment ago...what was it? It had sounded almost like a cry of pain.

She spotted an opening in the wall a short ways down. She knelt and crept toward it, paying little atten-tion to the dirt and rocks staining and catching at the delicate threads of her dress.

The opening had hinges welded into the old stone bricks; there had been a gate here once. It was gone now, and vines and brambles had filled in most of the space. But she could see through to the other side thanks to a few gaps, so she made herself as small and as quiet as possible amongst the overgrowth, and she watched.

And what she saw was more of what she'd seen from her bedroom window: *shadows*.

More strange shadows.

It looked almost as if the king was...*summoning* them. Or not fighting them off, at the very least. They moved swiftly and solidified into a distinguishable creature, just as before—only this time the creature was significantly smaller, and it moved on four legs instead of two.

That shadow beast leapt toward the king and twisted its way around his arm.

The king's eyes looked strangely empty. He swayed on his feet, nearly toppling over several times. Each time he started to topple, Sephia's breath caught in her throat. But every time, those strange shadows seemed to gather beneath him, catching him and forcing him back upright.

Was he unconscious?

I should help him, Sephia thought.

But she couldn't. She could scarcely breathe. Her entire body tingled with dangerous energy—the energy of that innate Shadow magic inside of her. It felt almost as if it was trying to rise up to play with these shadows before her.

She was afraid to move, terrified that any motion might shake that magic free.

She heard footsteps approaching.

So did the shadows, apparently; they scattered and disappeared into the normal and lifeless darkness of dusk.

Her magic settled, and Sephia rose quickly and scampered away to a different hiding place, not wanting anyone to spot her so close to the unconscious king. She found a more solid stretch of wall—one still close enough to listen— and she pressed her back to it. She briefly closed her eyes and breathed in deep breath after deep breath, trying to steady her pounding heart.

She considered going back to her room, but before she could move, she heard a familiar voice.

Tarron.

He greeted his brother, and Sephia held her breath until she heard the king greet him back in a somewhat groggy voice.

Not unconscious, then.

The prince's voice dropped to a whisper. Sephia kept her back pressed against the wall. She reached for one of the vines cascading down over that wall, squeezing tight, trying to steady herself.

She was too far away to hear most of the conversation between the king and the prince, and the few words that she *did* catch were in that confusing language of the Sun Court. But she could tell the prince was struggling to continue speaking in a hushed voice; it sounded like they were having an argument.

Curiosity got the better of her again. She gave that vine in her hand a quick tug. It stayed put. It was thick and sturdy, and there were several others like it—enough to support her weight as she hoisted herself up to peer over the wall once more.

She moved slowly, keeping herself half-hidden under a thick snarl of more vines. A bright red bug skittered out from beneath one of those vines and crawled over her wrist. She shivered. Swallowed down the urge to cry out and shake the pest away, and forced herself to focus on the king, on the places where the shadows had been so tightly wrapped around him a moment ago.

His back was to her, but his hands were still occasionally visible whenever he gestured. They looked as if they were still wrapped in shadows, grey and leathered and... shaking.

She gasped.

Tarron's gaze shifted toward her. Sephia tried to drop out of sight, but it was too late—

He had seen her.

And he moved too quickly for her to escape; in the next instant he was around the wall and then upon her, despite the king's insistence to leave her be.

"How long have you been hiding back there, *spying* on us?" Prince Tarron demanded.

"I wasn't spying," Sephia shot back. "I-I heard an argument, and I wanted to make sure everything was okay. If you didn't want people to listen, then you should have been quieter."

A muscle in his jaw twitched. "And did you hear anything that interested you, my dear *princess*?"

"No."

"Shame. Next time you should—"

"But I *saw* something."

He glared at her.

Sephia glared right back. "Your brother's hands are shaking. And they look...*dead.* And black and...diseased."

Tarron started to speak, but he seemed to lose track of his words as the king approached them.

King Deven glanced between the two of them. Sighed, and then held up one of those dark, disease-riddled hands. He spoke a single word—yet another that Sephia did not recognize—and let it linger in the silence. Warmth soon bloomed in the space all around them, and Sephia watched, speechless herself now, as the king's hands returned to normal. Even the shaking ceased, little by little, until it was barely noticeable.

He gave his younger brother a withering look as he tipped his head toward Sephia. "You can deal with this?" His tone suggested a question, but the look in his eyes led Sephia to believe that *yes* was the only acceptable answer.

Tarron nodded.

"Then I will take my leave," said the king, wearily, and then he did precisely this.

Once they were alone, Sephia swallowed hard and continued before the prince could speak: "They weren't shaking when we first arrived here. And they didn't look like *that*. I would have noticed, because he took my hand and walked me to my room." She glanced down at her own hands now—at her *sister's* hands. It still shocked her, the way that witch's magic had changed them, made them grey-tinted and wrinkled. She had to swallow to clear her throat again before she could continue: "He didn't catch it from *me*. Regardless of what your old doctor might have led you to believe, I am not contagious. I've never infected anyone."

Tarron took a deep breath. "No, he didn't catch it from you."

Sephia opened her mouth and shut it just as quickly.

She hadn't expected him to agree with her about...
well, *anything*.

"So..." she continued after her shock subsided, "he's
been using some sort of illusion magic to hide his illness?
Has he been hiding it for long?"

His skin had looked worse than hers—worse than
Nora's.

What did it mean?

Tarron didn't answer her; something in the distance
had caught his attention.

"What *else* are you hiding from me?" Sephia
demanded. "We aren't completely ignorant in my kingdom, you know. We know of the spells, the glamours and
the like that your kind use, and we—"

Suddenly Tarron was moving again, grabbing her
roughly by the arm and pulling her down a nearby path.

They came to a crossroads and hesitated. Sephia
started to pull away, but he stopped her with an impatient
look. His eyes darted to the left, and she followed his gaze
and saw that there were two young fae on the next path
over, pausing to pick fruit from a flowering tree.

"We need to find someplace more private," Prince
Tarron muttered. He changed direction and continued
dragging her along, until they finally came to an open
gate.

They left the gardens behind and made their way
down a steep hill, stopping once they reached a small
stream. The gently flowing water was a beautifully pecu-
liar shade of turquoise. There were little waterfalls, moss-
draped rocks, birds singing, butterflies with softly-
glowing wings...

It might have been an unbearably romantic spot under different circumstances.

Tarron glanced back at the gardens, and then he turned his back to them and breathed a quiet sigh. He looked as if he might be content to settle down beside the stream, doze off, and never talk about the king again.

Sephia was not as content.

"About your brother—"

"You will say *nothing* of what you saw," he said, calmly and coldly and without taking his eyes off the water.

"I can't just ignore it!"

"I think you'll find that you can. And you will. And you will also *lower your voice*. There are always ears listening around here, and though most of them know that my brother is sick, they..."

The space seemed to quiet and contract around them as he trailed off. Even the bird chatter stopped.

"...They don't know *how* sick?" Sephia guessed.

His silence made the answer clear enough.

They stood in that silence for several long, uncomfortable moments, until another thought occurred to Sephia, and she cautiously voiced it: "Is that the real reason you wanted that doctor to examine me? Because you believed that it might give you more answers? You believe we might be suffering the same illness?"

He averted his eyes. "Yes."

Sephia had a biting response already prepared, but something in his tone made her pause. It had sounded almost... vulnerable.

Vulnerable? That couldn't be right. And yet she had

never gone from furious to simply frustrated to almost...*sad* quite so fast. Why was she sad for him?

It was disorienting.

And also rather annoying.

"You could have just *told* me that was the reason behind it," she muttered. "I would have helped you. We could have had an actual conversation about the matter like two civilized beings."

He glanced back at her, his expression unreadable.

"But if you were doing it out of concern for your brother, then I..." She hesitated, hardly believing the words she was about to say. "I'll forgive you. This time."

"I don't need your forgiveness," he informed her. "And I don't need your help, either. Not for this."

Of course.

Sephia folded her arms over her chest, irritated that he'd swatted away her peace offering.

Why had she been foolish enough to extend it in the first place?

"All I need is for you to swear to me that you will ignore what you saw," said the prince, kneeling beside the stream and trailing his fingers through the water, "and again: that you will not speak of it."

"I could ignore the shaking and such, perhaps. But before you arrived, there were..."

He tilted his head back toward her.

She froze.

She wanted to claw her own voice box out. How *stupid* could she possibly be, to come so close to mentioning those shadows out loud?

Tarron pulled his hand from the water. Water slid

from his fingertips, *drip drip dripped* against the rocky ground, as his eyes narrowed on her. "What happened before I arrived?" he asked.

"N-nothing."

He straightened to his full, impressive height. "Leanora."

"Yes?"

"What exactly did you see?"

She couldn't think of a safe answer—one that didn't reveal that she could see those shadows that she was starting to suspect no one else in this realm could—so she kept her mouth shut.

The prince stepped toward her. "Do you want to have a *civilized* conversation about things or not?"

"I..."

"What are you keeping from me, hm?" He brought a hand up, brushed his knuckles across her cheek. The air around them began to warm. Her head felt unbearably heavy all of a sudden. All she wanted to do was rest it against his palm. To breathe in his pine and rainwater scent, and to close her eyes and listen to the soothing beat of his heart. And to tell him...

Tell him what?

She blinked.

Was he using magic against her?

"Don't do that," she warned.

"Do what?" He smiled.

It was not a friendly smile.

And she realized then that she didn't know the full extent of his magic. The thought sent a shiver of fear through her. Part of his Sun magic might have resided in

Leanora thanks to the bargain, yes, but that didn't mean he couldn't play with the small magic—the glamours and tricks— that *all* fae were capable of.

Could he force her to speak, somehow?

She needed to say something. Anything to break whatever spell he was attempting to weave around her.

"I'm not keeping anything from you," she lied, pulling away from his touch.

For a moment he looked as if he was considering reaching for her again.

And for a moment she *wanted* him to reach for her again.

More of that confusing magic at work, no doubt.

"I'm just not sure what I saw," she continued. "I could only tell that your brother wasn't feeling well, and so I was confused and afraid, and I...I think I might have simply been imagining the most terrible things."

"Imagining things?"

"But we could work together, as I said, and figure all of these things out."

His lips curled in what looked to be a combination of disgust and annoyance. "I told you: I don't need your help. All I need is for the magic that you possess to unlock mine, and then I will take care of my problems on my own. This marriage is nothing more than a means to an end."

She could practically feel the stone walls around her heart rebuilding, fortifying the places that had started to crack, and she was happy to let it happen. She much preferred the weight of stone to the warmth his touch— or his magic, or whatever— had briefly caused.

"Nothing more," she repeated.

"And nothing less. It will be...easier for you if you accept this now. I thought we already had an understanding?"

"We do," she said, icily.

Finally, he took a step back. But he was still watching her. Still expectant. Still *suspicious*.

Searching for another way to change the subject, she lifted the skirt of her dress, frowning at the gritty bits of dirt that had stained it during her garden adventure. "I fear I may have to change again before dinner."

"I don't believe dinner will be proceeding as planned anyhow," he said, distractedly. "I have...too many other things that need to be seen to this evening." He offered his arm. "Come. I'll see you safely back inside."

She lightly gripped his arm, and they walked together back to Solturne Hall. They said nothing. His muscles were tense and hard against her touch. It felt strange to move beside him like this, to feel his anxieties washing over her— almost as if they *were* close enough to share the weight of such things.

A means to an end, and nothing more, she reminded herself, fiercely.

Except that she *wasn't* the means he thought she was, either.

And the end she had planned for him was certainly different as well.

Her thoughts raced. Her stomach twisted over and over. The walk felt shorter than she'd expected it to, and once they reached the grand front doors of Solturne Hall,

Prince Tarron handed her off to one of the guards stationed there.

"Escort my bride back to her room," he commanded, "and see to it that she *stays* in that room for the evening."

The command annoyed her—the way he spoke of her like a troublemaking child— but something caught her attention before she could protest.

Another shadow beast, small but solid and certain, was sitting on a set of nearby steps.

Watching her.

But the moment she laid eyes on it, it turned and bounded out of sight.

CHAPTER 6

*T*hree days after the incident in the gardens, Tarron met his brother for dinner on the private veranda outside of the king's room.

"Doctor Elric's results are all inconclusive so far." He informed him, sinking down into the chair opposite of Deven, heavy with a feeling of defeat. "Useless old bastard."

King Deven chuckled. "You think everyone is useless."

"Not *everyone*." Tarron massaged his temples. He felt a headache coming on. "Just the ones who do nothing useful for me."

"Which is..."

"Okay. Fine. *Most* everyone."

Deven rolled his eyes. Smiled, and then he disappeared into his room for a moment.

Tarron squeezed his fingers more tightly against his forehead, still replaying the earlier conversation he'd had with Doctor Elric. To both his surprise and the doctor's, the tests Doctor Elric performed had found nothing that

S.M. GAITHER

linked Princess Leanora's ailments to King Deven's. They had similar symptoms, but nothing more.

It had taken Elric three days to perform those tests. Three more days of Deven potentially getting sicker—and with nothing to show for it.

And now Tarron *also* had his bride-to-be to worry about; her pallid appearance aside, she had been acting strange since their encounter in the gardens. Paranoid, almost. She rarely slept. She hardly ate. That odd scent he'd noticed at their first meeting still clung to her. But the doctor could find no medical reason for any of it.

Another person who defied explanation, same as his brother.

Just what he'd needed.

If he was the type to feel bitter about things, he might have been furious at the situation. Because here were the two beings in this realm that he was destined to be closest to, and *both* of them might end up dying on him sooner rather than later.

But bitterness wouldn't change anything, would it?

So it was a waste of time to feel it.

Deven returned, carrying two glasses of wine. He offered one to Tarron and then sipped at his own, looming over his brother for a moment with a thoughtful half-smile on his face.

The silence between them felt uncomfortably expectant, so Tarron cleared his throat, gave a slight smile of his own, and said, "I don't think *you're* useless, for what it's worth. Not entirely, anyway."

"I'm so flattered." Deven's crooked grin remained, though his eyes pinched with concern as he watched a flock of birds soaring by. "But what will you do when I'm gone? You may have to find someone else to rely on, you know. However useless you might think others are, you can't do everything yourself."

"I still aim to try."

Deven laughed.

Tarron didn't join in that laughter, because he wasn't joking. His brother might have been cavalier about his own death, but Tarron saw preparing for the possibility of it as a matter of duty.

He could admit that it was unavoidable, relying on others in some ways, but then they died—like his father and his mother, and like his brother and his wife-to-be perhaps—and then what? You ended up alone. So why not learn to do things on your own, too? It was not the character flaw his brother seemed to think it was; it was simply being practical.

"Independence has its merits, I suppose," Deven admitted. "But how *boring* would it be, living alone indefinitely?"

Tarron took another sip of his wine. He said nothing of his older brother's own independence, of the fact that the king himself was without a mate—though not by choice.

It was a difficult subject.

There had been an engagement, years ago, a queen-in-waiting... And then she'd gone on a diplomatic mission to Nocturne. Her ship had gone down in the middle of the Loral Sea, and her body had never been recovered.

Deven's lack of a queen was another reason some of

81

their subjects doubted his ability to rule. Some still thought that queen might be alive somewhere, despite Deven's insistence that their bond told him otherwise. Others thought foul play had been involved in her death, and that their king should have started a war to avenge it. But Deven was not the type to do anything of the sort; whatever wars he was fighting, he kept them to himself. Only Tarron saw his suffering.

And even then, it was only occasional glimpses of it.

"What does it matter, anyhow?" Tarron asked. "I won't be alone—because weren't you telling me just the other day that you don't plan on dying anytime soon?"

"I still don't." The king's tone was nonchalant, but his eyes were glazed and distant.

Silence again stretched between them, deep and uncertain now.

"That episode in the garden the other evening has to have worried you," Tarron finally ventured.

And for once, Deven didn't brush the concern aside.

"You haven't had an episode like that since..."

"Since the night of those shade beast sightings," Deven finished.

It had been three years since that night, and their court still did not entirely understand what had happened during it. They only agreed that there had been powerful magic involved, dark energies that had killed two of their kind and also caused Deven's strange ailment to flare to a nearly fatal point.

Many believed that a member of the rival Shadow Court had somehow slipped into their ranks, and that they had used their dark magic to reawaken the remnants of the gray belephor beast that had killed the former king and his queen. The true belephor did not reappear, but those reanimated pieces of it—*umbrae*, some called them — were enough to wreak plenty of havoc.

Several claimed to have seen those smaller beasts, and for weeks afterwards, accusations flew. Every other being in Solturne was suddenly a potential spy for the Shadow Court, or hiding Shadow magic themselves.

But in the end, they uncovered no concrete evidence, and to accuse that rival court of such atrocities without evidence would have resulted in broken treaties and all-out war.

So the incident lingered, unsolved, like a bruise that refused to heal.

But if it was happening again...

"Back to the matter of your *independence*," Deven began, and Tarron rolled his eyes, because here came the change of subject.

The king continued, undeterred: "It's been three days. Are you keeping track? Some members of the council are getting...antsy. They don't want you to be *independent*. They want a wedding."

"Let them get antsy."

Deven shook his head. "If the marriage—and your feelings—matter as little to you as you claim, then why not just get it over with? Surely it's just a matter of business? And I've never known you to dawdle when it came to business. The preparations have all been made. The court is simply waiting for you to say the word *go*."

Tarron shifted uncomfortably in his seat but said nothing.

The king lifted his gaze to the sky, appeared to lose himself in thought for a moment, and then he said, "She still isn't showing much affection toward you, I'm guessing?"

"No. Can you blame her?"

Deven cut his eyes back to his little brother, smiling again.

Tarron grimaced. "Why are you grinning at me like that?"

"Because," said the king—and that was all he said, no matter how hard Tarron glared at him.

"You're incredibly annoying," said Tarron, sinking deeper into his chair and closing his eyes. The headache was officially here, now.

Deven dropped into the chair across from him; the sound of its feet scraping across the stone tile was cringe-inducing. "You might not care about *your* feelings, but is there a chance you're starting to care about hers? And perhaps you don't want to rush her?"

Tarron yawned.

"Look at you, caring about another so deeply."

"Be quiet."

"I'm so happy for you."

"*Quiet*, I said."

"You know what? I'm going to have the servants help you out." Deven clapped his hands together. "I know—perhaps they can deliver some flowers on your behalf? Or some other gift? Something so she won't realize you have all the charm of a dead and flattened frog. Surely with myself and all of our servants' powers combined, we could fool her into thinking you're a romantic soul. That you're passionate, and perhaps worthy of—"

"I'm going to passionately chuck this at your head if you don't stop talking," Tarron warned, popping one eye open and giving his wine glass a shake—though he was fighting off a laugh now. Deven *was* incredibly annoying, as he'd said, but his brother's good humor was also infectious at times.

"I was only trying to help," said Deven, still grinning.

Tarron finally allowed himself to laugh. "I suppose I do need all the help I can get, don't I?"

"Cheers to that." The king lifted his glass and clinked it against Tarron's.

Dinner arrived a moment later. They spoke no more of marriage or illnesses or romantic gestures after that, and the evening pressed peacefully onward, for which Tarron was grateful.

HOURS LATER, once dinner was finished and his brother was thoroughly, happily drunk and ready to sleep, the prince retreated to his own room.

He intended to head straight for the small alcove of that room—one that contained a spare desk, which was littered with various reports and record-keeping books that he needed to look over. But after stepping into his quiet bedroom, he instead found himself drawn to the hallway to his left.

Just down that hall, in a room that mirrored his own in size and grandeur, was his bride-to-be.

She was in there brooding, most likely. Or frustrating the servants with her refusal to sleep and eat properly. Or perhaps feeding her food to Ketzal—she had developed quite the bond with the griffin over the past few days, mostly because of her unrestrained offerings of sugary treats.

As if that little beast needs more spoiling.

A wry smile threatened to spread across Tarron's face. He fought it off. With one last lingering look in the direction of his desk, he slipped off his coat and draped it over the footboard of his bed, and then he headed for the princess's room.

A guard was stationed at the end of the connecting hallway. There was one at each of the room's entrances. It was less about keeping her inside, and more about keeping the more curious palace dwellers *outside*. Because it was just as Deven had mentioned earlier— certain members of their court *were* getting antsy. And he didn't want them harassing her.

The guard—Malark, was his name—bowed low as Tarron approached.

"How is my bride-to-be this evening?"

Malark seemed startled by the question. Maybe because of the distance Tarron had been keeping from that bride over these past few days.

"Well?" Tarron prompted.

"Sleeping soundly, Your Highness."

"Good." Something that felt suspiciously like relief washed over Tarron. He'd been more worried about her than he'd realized, perhaps. Worried enough that he even briefly considered going into the room to check on her.

He wanted to see her, to personally make certain she was safe and comfortable.

He wanted to see her.

Why?

Let it be. You have other things to worry about.

"You may take your leave," he told the guard. "I don't plan on leaving my room for the remainder of the night; I can see to her safety on my own."

The guard left with another bow, making his way down the hall and exiting through Tarron's room. Tarron watched him go, and then he looked back to that door that would lead him to the princess.

A door.

That was all that separated him from that princess, and yet it felt like it could have been an entire ocean.

Shaking his head, he left the door closed and went back to his own room.

The stack of papers waiting on his desk was tall; his brother was even more behind with these things than he usually was, and so Tarron had offered to help. He had started this task earlier, in his proper study on the floor below this one, but he hadn't finished it. And it could have waited until morning, but Tarron was eager to get back to it.

His brother accused him of being addicted to work, but Tarron didn't see it as pure *work*. He enjoyed it too much—the numbers, the notes, the written correspondence with the various lords and ladies of their realm. He liked making lists. He liked checking things off, and wrestling things into order and keeping them there. It made him feel calm and in control.

It calmed him enough that, eventually, his mind was going blissfully numb. His eyelids fluttered open and shut. The stacks of parchment became tempting pillows, and his head grew heavy, dragging him downward.

Just a quick nap...

A loud crash woke him—one that came from Leonora's room.

He was on his feet in an instant, racing through the narrow passage to that room. He flung open the door and stopped, taking in the sight before him.

The bedside lamp was on the floor, along with a water glass that was now in countless sharp and shiny pieces. She had knocked it all over—and no wonder, with the way she was flailing about in her sleep. She looked like she was caught in the throes of a terrible nightmare. But other than that, she appeared to be safe.

He exhaled slowly.

His first instinct, again, was to let her be. If she was to be his wife, then it meant that there were far more frightening things on her horizon than nightmares. Fae politics, for starters, were not for the faint of heart.

And yet he couldn't seem to make himself move.

What was it that kept him there, staring at her, waiting for a sign that she had escaped her bad dreams? Pity? No; he rarely bothered to show pity, and she didn't strike him as the type that would *want* him to show it, besides.

Something else was making him stay.

And then something else made him walk toward her.

Something else made him kneel at her bedside, take the ring from his finger, and slip it over hers. It was an old family heirloom, that ring, and its calming magic was powerful. It shrank and grew to fit the wearer; he watched as it glowed faintly for a moment before settling onto her much smaller, more delicate finger.

Warmth blossomed in the space around them.

She inhaled deeply, greedily—as if she had just resurfaced from a near-drowning. After several gasping breaths, a shudder went through her entire body, and then she began to relax. She was still tossing and turning, but the movements were less violent now.

Tarron took hold of her arm, trying to keep her still. His hand slid down to her wrist, felt the alarmingly quick pulse there. Every pounding beat drove his powerful senses a little more wild; the storm of sound and movement and scent that surrounded her was chaotic and hard to sort through at first.

But after a minute of kneeling beside her, he became aware of individual things. Quieter things. The pout of her lips. The stubborn furrow of her brow. And beneath that odd scent of hers was...another scent. A less nauseating one. It reminded him, however faintly, of honey and roses.

Her pulse finally slowed.

And then, strangely enough, his seemed to slow as well— almost as if it wanted to match hers.

He let go of her arm and studied her for a moment longer.

Just putting the ring on her had been enough to settle her; he hadn't even needed to speak that ring's stronger magic into existence. Not surprising though, was it? Humans were weak, and so even weak magic was enough to overtake her mind and calm it—more proof that he was right not to let his feelings for her grow; he wasn't convinced she was strong enough to last at his side.

He stood up and started for his own room, but paused in the doorway and glanced at his stolen bride one last time. She had kicked most of her blankets onto the floor, he noticed, and now she was curling into a ball, clearly shivering. Cold, even with the warmth of his ring's magic.

With a sigh, he doubled back and covered her up once more.

CHAPTER 7

*S*ephia felt as if she was being cradled by a cloud. She was drifting through a warm, bright place somewhere outside of reality, and she didn't want to wake up.

When was the last time she had slept—truly slept—like this?

But it didn't last.

All too soon, something was nagging at her, trying to rouse her.

Pain.

It spasmed through her hand. Just a slight tingling at first, but then it started to warm. Her skin felt tighter, scorched down to her bones, and soon the heat was so intense that she couldn't catch her breath. The clouds cradling her became *flames*—

Her eyes blinked open.

She immediately found the source of the burning: There was a strange ring around her finger.

S.M. GAITHER

And she couldn't get it off.

She pulled and pulled, but it only held tighter. Burned hotter. It felt as if flames were siphoning from the ring's sapphire center and into her skin, as if it might set her entire body ablaze if she didn't get it *off*. She kept pulling, wrestling and rolling about on the bed. Her legs tangled in the blankets, and then she pitched over the side of that bed and toppled to the floor.

Ow.

She must have cried out before waking, because as she pushed herself up off the floor, suddenly her room flooded with people—with guards and servants bursting through both doors, asking what was wrong.

And then the prince himself arrived.

Their eyes met.

The moment felt suspended and surreal; he looked half-asleep and more disheveled than she'd ever seen him, and something about that appearance—compared to his usual stiff, otherworldly perfection—was strange.

He looked almost...*human.*

But still better looking than any human she'd ever met. Her breath caught in her throat as he stepped toward her. How did he manage to still look so beautiful, even with messy hair and eyes heavy with sleep?

Then the ring pulsed with more of that borderline painful, burning energy, and fury overtook the fluttering in her heart.

He's not beautiful.

He's monstrous.

Because this ring was the same one she'd seen him wearing before, she was certain, and it was clearly another shackle like the bracelet she wore—except she hadn't been awake to give consent for this particular shackle.

"I need to speak with you," she told the prince, fighting to keep her voice level. "And I want everyone else to *leave*."

The guards and servants all looked to the prince.

Prince Tarron breathed slowly in, exhaled even more slowly, and then gave a single, curt nod. "As she commands."

After a moment of confused hesitation, the others obediently filed out.

Once they were alone, Prince Tarron wasted no time closing the distance between them. "What in the name of the three gods were you *screaming* about—"

"*This!*" She jabbed her finger—and the ring—accusingly in his direction, nearly poking him in the eye as she did. "It won't come off!"

He took another deep breath. Reached for the ring. Tapped it. Whispered a single, strange word under his breath, and then slipped the ring off— with ease— and said, "It adjusts to fit the wearer securely. If you had simply relaxed, you could have pulled it off yourself."

She stared at the unassuming piece of jewelry, still not quite believing how easily he'd taken it off. After swallowing to clear the dryness in her throat, she asked, "And why was *I* wearing it? I didn't go to sleep with it on."

"I put it on you while you were sleeping."

Her temper flared as hot as those clouds in her dream-turned-nightmare. "It's magical, isn't it? I could feel it starting to burn me. I could feel its power sinking into my skin, and if this is some sort of trick that—"

"I put it there as a ward against whatever nightmares you were having."

"It—oh."

He yawned. "*Oh* indeed."

She narrowed her eyes at his blasé tone. "Nightmares," she repeated. "How did you…?"

"You were flailing around like a fish out of water last night." He nodded toward her nightstand. "You broke the glass. You ruined the lamp, too."

She followed his gaze, searching for that lamp, for that glass that had been filled with water.

Both had been replaced.

"I was only trying to help you," the prince said.

"Well it didn't feel like help," she grumbled. "It felt… suffocating. Strange."

He gave her a curious look. "It's Sun magic. It shouldn't have felt strange to you."

Panic rose in her, sudden and sharp, making her words painful to get out: "It didn't… I mean—it *did* feel like Sun magic. I recognized it as such, *obviously*. But it was just more powerful than the Sun magic that I'm used to feeling, that's all."

He was so frustratingly good at walling off his expressions that she couldn't tell whether he was suspicious of her lie or not.

She cautiously extended her hand to take the ring back. He deposited it in her outstretched palm without comment. She tried not to wince as it touched her skin, as she braced for more burning.

"Sun magic is life-sustaining, protective, warming..." he trailed off, watching her in that expectant way of his. "This particular ring is enchanted in such a way that it provides the wearer with clarity and calmness in their mind. I assumed it would settle any nightmares."

"Yes, of course." She tried to sound confident. "But is that really *all* this particular ring does?"

He nodded. "It's an old family heirloom; my great-grandfather forged it as a gift to his first-born."

She turned it over and over in her hand. It was still tingling with heat. Was it reacting to the Shadow magic buried inside of her? She half-expected it to burn a hole through her palm and release that magic, to reveal the truth of her right then and there.

Clarity indeed.

After a moment, she caught her breath enough to glance up and ask, "And is it true that fae can't lie?"

He snorted. "Where did you hear that?"

"My old caretaker—Nana Rosa. She was always telling us stories about such things."

"Stories can be misleading."

"Well? Is it true, then?"

"The truth is a tricky thing."

Sephia fixed him with a glare. "Yes; Nana Rosa *also* said that fae don't give true answers whenever they can help it."

"She sounds like an intelligent woman," Tarron dead-panned. "Now—did she teach you how to act when people are trying to *help* you?"

Her heart threatened to do that annoying, fluttering thing once more.

He'd been trying to help her.

Was he telling the truth?

"You slept better than you had on previous nights, did you not?" he asked.

She wanted to argue, but she couldn't. He was right. She had woken up more refreshed than she had in a long time—even in spite of her sleep's nightmarish ending.

"I'm victorious in one battle, it seems," said the prince in response to her silence. "Now if only you would eat something, I would consider myself quite the strategist."

She could still think of nothing to say.

How annoying.

"On that note," said the prince, victoriously, "I propose we have breakfast together, since we're already up."

Sephia only just kept herself from cringing at the suggestion.

She couldn't cringe; she needed to do this. She needed to spend more time with her target, both to learn more about him *and* to make certain he wasn't growing too suspicious of her.

The only problem was her *own* suspicions.

She still didn't entirely trust the food being served in this palace; the only reason she hadn't starved yet was because a package had arrived for her the day after she came to Solturne Hall, and—to her great surprise—the king had allowed her to have that package. It had been from Nora. And her little sister had been smart enough to include a few edible delights along with a letter and a few other reminders of her true home.

She couldn't rely on that small stash of food forever, though.

"Well?" he pressed.

"Fine," she agreed. "But only under one condition."

He looked disgruntled—likely because he wasn't used to other people making the rules. After a moment, however, he gave her that curious look of his and asked, "And what is this...*condition*?"

"I want to cook it."

He looked almost as mortified as he had on the day they'd first met, when she'd suggested bringing her own luggage to Solturne Hall. "That isn't...necessary."

"I know it isn't."

"I have perfectly capable cooks. If there are certain instructions you feel compelled to give, it's only a matter of directing—"

"Yes, but I *enjoy* cooking for myself. And for others."

"Did you not have enough servants to do such things for you back in the Central Palace?"

"I did."

He still appeared skeptical.

"But I was a better cook than most of them."

He scoffed.

"You don't believe me? Allow me to prove it, why don't you?"

He lifted a brow at the competitive slant her tone had taken on. "Very well," he said, yawning again. Perhaps he was just too tired to argue for once. It was still strange to her, seeing him so bedraggled and so much less...severe. She had been starting to think he never let his guard down, even to sleep.

This is the perfect opportunity to get closer to him— while that guard is down.

"Oh, and one more condition," she said.

His gaze tracked to the ceiling, as if petitioning some heavenly being for strength.

"You have to cook with me."

He shook his head, though it seemed to be more in disbelief than refusal.

"Unless you're afraid you won't be able to keep up with me?" she prompted.

"I'm terrified."

"Don't worry; I'm an excellent teacher."

"You're also very modest, I've noticed."

She found herself speechless again. Because was it her imagination, or had his tone turned almost...playful?

My imagination, she told herself, stubbornly.

But as he headed to his room to dress, he glanced back at her one last time.

And she thought she saw the beginning of a smile cross his face.

AN HOUR LATER, Sephia had washed and dressed, and she was standing in the main kitchen of Solturne Hall.

It was such a massive space that she spent several minutes simply wandering from one end of it to the next, marveling at the vast assortment of pots and pans, at the seemingly endless amount of fully-stocked shelves, at the ovens that numbered so many she kept losing count.

It connected to an outdoor section that featured even *more* ovens, these ones made of brick and surrounded by various types of neatly-stacked wood. Fresh fruits and vegetables hung in rows of baskets along two edges of this outer section. There was an entire raised garden along the third edge, and she had never seen such beautiful, fresh-looking herbs as the ones growing in that garden.

A chef is only as good as her ingredients, Chef Talos— her cooking tutor back in Middlemage—used to say.

And these ingredients looked good enough that they could have made a decent chef out of just about anybody.

In short, she was in heaven.

Even if she *was* sharing the pristine space with a still sleepy and grumpy-faced fae.

"So, um, first things first," she began in response to Tarron's impatient staring. "We need to gather our ingredients, and our tools..." She bounced from one basket and drawer to the next, collecting things. She hummed to herself as she went, growing increasingly happier in spite of Tarron's grumpiness, and in spite of the overall mess she was in.

She was always happy when she was cooking.

Tarron continued to watch her. She didn't pay him much attention, but his gaze was slowly softening, she thought, as she kept humming. And when she pulled a pair of tongs out and absently snapped them together, he cleared his throat and asked: "Why did you do that?"

"Do what?"

"Click those...whatever they are... together?"

"They're tongs." Sephia looked at the utensil in her hand, feeling suddenly mystified herself. "And I don't know," she said with a shrug. "It's one of the rules of cooking, though—you have to give tongs a few test clicks whenever you pull them out of the drawer."

He gave her a dubious look. "Should I be writing these rules down?"

She almost laughed, but caught herself and switched back to her head chef voice. "No— just pay attention."

She found a cutting board and started to dice up vegetables.

"What are we making, precisely?" He sounded genuinely curious now, which for some reason made her nervous.

"Um...some sort of egg scramble, maybe? Are those pygmy hen eggs over there?"

He nodded.

"Hand them here."

He did, still watching her uncertainly, as if he thought she might be concocting a deadly potion of some sort.

"What? I'm just making it up as I go, that's all."

He looked mortified again, but he recovered more quickly this time. He dutifully went back to handing her ingredients and tools. "Do you need these?"

"Maybe," she said, taking a ring of measuring spoons from him only to toss them aside.

She worked out how to light the smallest and least-intimidating looking oven first, and then she found a cooling barrel full of something that at least *looked* like butter. She scooped some of it out and plopped it into a saucepan.

"That is...a lot," Tarron commented.

"You can never have too much butter. Write *that* down if you like; it's perhaps the most important rule."

The pan sizzled and popped as she added her diced vegetables, and the air soon filled with the scent of onions and peppers. She tossed in a myriad of spices she found, humming to herself again, completely focused on her sautéing ingredients, determined to get their texture just right.

When she finally looked up, Tarron was frowning.

"What is it?"

"You didn't measure those spices," he accused.

"I did."

He glanced at the still-perfectly-clean measuring spoons.

"I measured it all with my heart."

His eyes narrowed.

She stifled another laugh.

He canted his head. "Ah. You were telling a joke."

"I was." She looked away—hopefully before the blush she felt in her cheeks grew too noticeable.

Why was she joking around with him like this?

She cleared her throat. "I get the impression that you like it when things are neat and organized."

He didn't object.

"But cooking is an art, not a science. And sometimes art is messy." She wiped at a bit of sweat on her brow, realizing too late that there was still a glob of that buttery substance on her hand.

He seemed to be considering her statement carefully. His eyes lingered for a moment on the streak of butter she'd left on her forehead, and then he took a towel and wiped away that *mess* just as carefully.

She felt a bit lightheaded at his touch. She quickly

searched the kitchen for her next task. "We'll add the eggs in a few minutes, but while those vegetables finishing cooking, I'll make a berry sauce for our toast. And we'll need to light another burner, get some water boiling for tea…"

"I can manage to boil water, I think."

"Let's see it, then," she said with an amused smirk.

He left her and went to another stovetop.

Her lightheadedness remained—maybe it was the heat and her lack of food, not his touch—but she persevered, and went about her sauce-making.

A few minutes later and she was nearly finished, and looking forward to finally eating something that was safe and of her own making. Her eyes nearly welled with happy tears at the thought.

But then she heard: "Why is it smoking so much?"

She turned just as flames sprouted from underneath the tea kettle.

"Oh…*okay*, gods, there's not supposed to be that much fire, here, move—" She snatched up a pot lid. Raced over to Tarron, knocked the kettle aside, and then attempted to smother the flames with the lid. "There must have been oil residue or something on the—"

"I'm going to summon somebody to deal with this," he insisted, his tone more annoyed than frantic even as several larger flames licked their way out from underneath the pot lid.

"No, I've got it under control!"

"*Do* you?"

Sephia was unfazed by his doubt. "There's no salt in this kitchen, is there?"

He made a disgusted face.

Right. The fae don't like salt. At least some of Nana Rosa's stories were true, it seemed. And this truth was especially unfortunate, considering how quickly salt could douse a fire.

"Okay, next plan: I need a damp towel or something. Quickly!"

The flames were growing steadily out of control. Panic still did not make an appearance within Tarron's expression, but he *did* move more quickly than Sephia had ever seen him move.

He disappeared but returned to her side within seconds, carrying several wet towels, and together they tossed them over the fire and turned it into nothing more than steam and smoke.

Sephia waved that noxious cloud away from them. "There...see?" she said in-between coughs. "We didn't need any help."

"Yes— it seems you have plenty of experience putting out kitchen fires, for some reason."

She grimaced as a series of memories flashed through her mind. "I... I might have caught a kitchen on fire once or twice in the past."

Or five or ten times, maybe...

Tarron shifted one of the damp towels and wrinkled his nose as another cloud of smokey steam erupted. "I thought you said you were an expert?"

"Yes, well, it happens to the best of us." She went back to the other stove. Her sauce had bubbled over. With a sigh, she started to clean this mess up as well.

She sensed Tarron behind her a moment later, come to inspect the second disaster for himself.

"Messy, like I said." She tilted her head toward him and offered a sheepish smile that he didn't return. "And you've officially made *your* first cooking mess, so..."

He glanced over his shoulder at that still-steaming mess. "So I'm making art, now?"

She tensed at the growling tone of his voice.

His eyes were shining strangely. From the steam and smoke, perhaps, but there was something else in them as well—an emotion she couldn't quite name. She held her breath, waiting for it to erupt into his usual pompous, arrogant irritation.

But then he *laughed*.

The sound was...intoxicating. Like a warm breeze on a crisp spring day, it washed over her skin and settled there like a spell.

And soon, she was grinning herself.

She turned her attention back to her berry sauce attempt. Slid a finger through it and then tasted it. It wasn't completely ruined, she decided; bits of it had caramelized with the excess heat, which made for a texture that was...*interesting*, at least.

"Disastrous," Tarron said, gazing once more at the pile of soggy, smoke-stained towels. He looked back at her after a moment, and then to the bubbled-over sauce and the sticky trail of it covering her hand. "Simply disastrous."

"It isn't all a disaster," she insisted. "Here—taste this and see for yourself."

It happened so quickly that neither of them realized

what they were doing until it was too late; one moment Sephia was running her finger along the edge of the sticky pan. The next, her body was nearly flush with the prince's, backed against the messy stove. Her finger was raised, and then his lips were against it, softly tasting the tangy yet sweet—and slightly scorched—concoction.

Oh.

Her mind momentarily blanked. Her mouth couldn't form words. Her fingers seemed to move on their own, trailing along his lips, tracing the spaces that she suddenly wanted to press her own lips against. A pleasant shiver cascaded through her.

What was she doing?

She'd wanted to get closer to him, but this...

This was *too* close.

And yet she didn't pull away. She stood there, hardly daring to breathe, even as he reached for her hand and pulled it away from his lips.

His fingers laced through hers. Squeezed. Then his grip loosened just enough to allow his thumb to trace her palm as she'd traced his mouth. His fingers stilled against her. His hooded gaze lingered on her lips, and for a moment she thought he might kiss her.

"That..." he breathed.

The low tone of his voice sent another tingle through her. She found herself leaning closer, listening. *Hoping,* maybe.

"...is incredibly sticky," he finished, pulling his hand away from hers and studying the bits of sauce that had been transferred to his hand from hers.

She snorted. "At least I didn't start a fire."

He laughed again—another taste that proved more dizzying and intoxicating than the first, because now he was close enough to her that the sound vibrated over her flushed skin.

She took a step back.

She *had* to.

"You started a fire trying to boil water," she said, shaking her head. "That's so...*impressive*." It still felt risky, teasing him like this when she knew how quickly he could turn cold—but she wanted to hear him laugh again.

Her risk-taking earned her a wry smile. "Don't tell anyone," he said.

She smiled back. "Your secret's safe with me."

He stepped back, putting even more space between them.

She felt a strange desire to pull him back, but she resisted it.

After a moment of gazing around the kitchen, he said, "I know you likely have me pegged as a fool who can't do anything without my servants, but I actually prefer doing most things for myself. Cooking, however..."

"Perhaps it's best you *do* leave that to those servants, as you said."

His smile turned crooked. "Or I'll simply leave it to my wife, if that pleases her. I'll set one of the tables in the garden for us in the meantime, shall I?"

She nodded, numbly.

My wife.

Her heart had skipped several beats at those words.

But it should have skipped, shouldn't it? In fear. In

regret and anxiety over this delicate, dangerous mission —at the thought of failing that mission and actually being the forever-trapped wife of this mysterious, monstrous fae prince.

Only it felt like... like something *else* had made it skip.

Something traitorous.

CHAPTER 8

When Sephia carried their food outside a short time later, she found that Tarron had wandered off to the adjacent gardens in search of flowers. While she arranged the plates and food, he arranged those flowers in a pitcher in the table's center. He worked without comment, all the while still wearing his usual brooding, serious frown. He appeared determined not to fail at this the way he'd failed at boiling water.

Sephia watched him with a bemused little smile on her face.

He'd given her a ring, and now flowers, too.

Monsters can give gifts, she stubbornly reminded herself. *It doesn't truly make them any less monstrous. You still need to be careful.*

They ate in relative silence, recovering from the various kitchen catastrophes and enjoying the warm sunshine. Several servants checked in on them while they dined. Tarron waved them all away, telling them he wanted to eat with his bride in private, which made Sephia's confused thoughts race even faster.

Rude awakening aside, this morning had felt entirely too...*nice.*

Because of that privacy Tarron requested, once they were finished, the mess in the kitchen remained. Sephia tried to help take care of it—her mentor had always taught her that cleaning up was part of cooking, like it or not—but this was where the prince finally drew the line.

My wife can be a cook, he insisted, *but not a kitchen slave.*

So they left the mess to the servants and then strolled together through Solturne Hall. They were close enough to hold hands, but Sephia didn't trust herself to do this. She kept her arms wrapped tightly around her middle as they walked.

They passed several others—nobles and servants alike—who bowed and then watched them with unabashed curiosity. Sephia did not focus on their faces, but rather on the twists and turns of the hallways, and on the various rooms they passed. She needed to better memorize this place for practical, related-to-her-mission reasons.

Nevertheless, her eyes kept being drawn to less practical things. To the gold-framed works of art. To the wall sconces that flickered with various-colored flames. To the soaring ceilings, the marble statues tucked in seemingly every nook, and the windows that gave glimpses of gardens so beautiful they made her mouth fall open.

She had scarcely left her room over the past three days, and never so early as this; the morning light bathed things in a glow that made her feel as if she had never woken up from her cloud-filled dreams. She had grown up in a palace of her own. She was used to splendor. But...

What would it be like to wake up every morning and stroll through these halls?

Why did this feel so different from home?

Because it's drenched in dangerous fae magic, came the harsh reply from her smarter, more sensible side.

They reached one of the spiraling staircases that led to the second floor, and Tarron paused at the foot of it and said, "You were right, earlier, you know."

"About what?"

"I like order. I like...calm."

She glanced over at him.

"And you are..."

"Chaos?" she supplied.

He shrugged.

"Yet another thing Nana Rosa used to say." Homesickness surged through her. She averted her eyes so he couldn't see any emotion that might be welling up in them. They climbed the steps together, and when they reached the top, Sephia found more words spilling out from her before she could stop them: "My sister was the calm one."

"Was she?"

Sephia bit her lip, sealing her reply inside. It felt like she was revealing too much of herself already, and she was hesitant to share any more.

But then again, he didn't know their separate personalities, did he? She still *looked* like Nora, and that was what mattered. It wouldn't hurt anything if she acted like Sephia. He wouldn't know the difference. Right?

The only question was, why did she suddenly *want* him to know the real her?

"You miss her terribly, I'd imagine," said the prince. "Your sister, I mean."

She pictured Nora's face. Tried to remember the cadence of her voice, the sparkle of her laugh. It had only been days since she'd heard these things, but it felt like much longer. A lump formed in her throat, but she managed a nod.

Tarron took her hand, and they continued their walk.

She wanted to pull away—she didn't like all of these tumbling, complicated feelings she was having, and his touch made them worse—but she kept holding on to him. They had made surprising progress this morning. He was starting to trust her a bit, maybe.

Which is precisely what I need from him.

"When things have all settled down," he said, "perhaps we can arrange a visit."

Sephia slowed to a stop, staring at him, unsure of what to say.

"We'll think on it," he said, giving her hand a small squeeze. He started to pull her back into motion, but at that moment they both noticed they were being watched; a small group of elegant-looking females were gathered at the end of the hall, whispering amongst themselves while occasionally tossing a not-so-subtle glance at the prince.

"A lot of staring this morning," Sephia commented, stiffly.

"They're just...curious. Surprised to see us holding hands, perhaps. Not all of them are convinced our wedding ceremony is going to happen."

Sephia frowned.

"They'll be kinder toward you in time," Tarron assured her.

She nodded despite the uneasy feeling in the pit of her stomach. She didn't want to care what they thought of her or her relationship with their prince. She had never made a habit of caring what people thought about her.

But she *had* to care this time, if only because she couldn't afford to have anyone doubting her.

She was the Stolen Bride of Middlemage. The Peace Offering. The Treaty Keeper. She was playing a part, and perhaps she hadn't been playing it well enough.

She took a deep breath. Her eyes focused on those distant onlookers, and the words floated out of her on a nervous, shaking breath: "Kiss me."

Tarron dropped her hand, as if in surprise, but otherwise didn't reply.

Sephia steeled herself and tilted her face back toward him. Her breath caught when she saw the way he was looking at her—like she'd... *awakened* something. Something dark and hungry and dangerous. It frightened her.

But she couldn't back down now.

"Kiss me and make them believe that I'm your bride-to-be," she whispered.

He hesitated for such a long moment that she thought he would deny her.

Then he lifted a hand. Brushed it across her cheek. Threaded his fingers through her hair and wrapped them around her head, holding her still, forcing her gaze to his. His grip was powerful. Possessive. She thought of all the stories she'd heard of the fae's insatiable lust, of the brutal ways they claimed both willing and unwilling lovers, and her heart thudded painfully quick in her chest.

But though Tarron's grip was powerful, and his strength unyielding as he backed her against the wall, his lips were surprisingly feather-light when they pressed against her own. It was a gentle, chaste kiss. Over in a fiery instant, but the feel of it lingered even as he leaned away.

She braced a hand against the wall behind her, steadying herself. Her body was tense, her heart still racing, and the prince seemed amused by this.

"If you want it to look convincing," he said, the words falling quiet and hot against her ear as he leaned forward again, "then you should relax."

She tried. She wanted to relax into him, into another kiss that was deeper, harder than the last. But the thought of doing so was entirely too tempting in ways that it shouldn't have been.

She was losing her head over a simple kiss, and it was...embarrassing.

This was supposed to be a trick to fool onlookers.

And yet *she* was the one who suddenly felt like a fool.

The sound of approaching footsteps rescued her from her foolishness.

Someone was calling for the prince a moment later; Sephia turned to see a silver-haired fae approaching— one of his senior advisors, Tarron informed her before excusing himself to go speak with that advisor.

He returned to her side after a minute, his eyes distant and his mouth drooping in the corners.

That frown...was it only because he was disappointed that they'd been interrupted?

Or was it something worse?

Why did she suddenly ache to know what was troubling him?

"I have some business to attend to," he told her. He hesitated, and then added, "It could wait. If you..."

"No," she said, perhaps too quickly. "I mean—I'm fine. You should go take care of whatever you need to. I wanted to go back to my room and rest, anyhow."

He searched her face for a moment—for what, she wasn't sure—and then he nodded.

Sephia walked the rest of the way to her room alone. She kept her head high and ignored all of the eyes still watching her, and the whispers that started once she'd passed by. Those whispers were louder, and the occasional laugh braver, now that the prince wasn't at her side.

She was grateful to finally reach the sanctuary of her room.

But unfortunately, more eyes fell upon her as soon as she stepped inside that room; a half dozen servants were waiting for her.

"My lady," said the one closest to her, sweeping into a low bow. "We've changed your linens, cleaned every surface, aired the room out, and we are here to provide you with anything else you may require—"

"I require nothing but privacy," Sephia told them as politely as she could.

They didn't budge.

She wondered if they were under orders to not leave her alone. Her gaze narrowed at the thought, and she fixed it on each of servants in turn.

The woman who'd spoken to her stepped closer. Her mouth pressed into a thin little line. It reminded Sephia of the way Nana Rosa's used to twist right before she launched into a lecture—and so it hardly fazed Sephia.

"Leave," she ordered. "Now."

The woman huffed a foreign word under her breath, but then she curtsied quickly and motioned for the others to follow her out of the room.

Once they were gone, Sephia closed the door and sank back against it. Memories of the morning flashed through her mind, and she cursed into the silence settling around her.

She had meant to search the kitchen for things she could use as potential weapons, for ways she might mask poison in the prince's food. She had meant to have more useful conversations with that prince—something that would have revealed more of his weaknesses.

Instead, she had ended up laughing with him. Kissing him. *Enjoying his company*.

"Idiot," she said to herself. With a sigh, she pushed away from the door and wandered toward the bed. She picked up the letter Nora had sent. Her eyes misted over as she read it for perhaps the hundredth time.

She could hear her twin's voice in her head, gently rebuking her: *You're too hard on yourself, Sephia. Let's focus on the things you've accomplished.*

Sephia tried to.

She had made it over three days now without her true identity being discovered. The prince had given her a ring—one with protective powers, thus leaving himself less protected. That prince seemed to be growing less hostile toward her, and that counted for something, didn't it? It would make moving around the palace and gathering more information easier.

And yet all of these things counted for nothing when she thought about how she'd felt when he'd kissed her.

It had felt entirely too good.

Too *real.*

Breathing out another curse, she folded Nora's letter and placed it on the nightstand, next to the ring Tarron had given her.

She'd left that ring on this nightstand earlier—pretended to forget it—because she was afraid of what would happen if she wore it too long. But now she couldn't stop herself from picking it up and sliding it onto her finger.

It still burned against her skin, but she left it on. The prince would want to see her wearing it, she told herself. Another way to build the trust between them. And perhaps it would help her keep her Shadow magic buried more deeply inside of her.

With this comforting thought settling her mind, she

plopped down on her bed and curled up with one of the overstuffed pillows. Before long, her eyes closed and she was drifting off.

SOMETHING STARTLED her back awake a short time later: A feeling that she was being *watched*.

She bolted upright, clutching the pillow to her chest. She scanned the room, expecting a servant, or perhaps a mischievous Ketzal—but the space was empty save for herself. The windows were closed. The doors were shut.

"Nothing there," she whispered, trying to reassure herself.

But she still *sensed* something. Bumps had shivered to life across her skin. Her blood felt cold, her body lighter. It was the same sensation she felt whenever her Shadow magic started to rise to the surface.

The same sensation she'd felt when she'd encountered that shadow beast attacking the king.

She recognized that dark energy. There was no mistaking it. And after a moment of sitting with it, a possibility occurred to her: The Sun magic possessed by the king and his followers... did it blind them to those shadows that were stalking the halls of this place?

She yanked the prince's ring off and tossed it back onto the nightstand...and then she gasped.

Because her suspicions were instantly proven correct: The same shadowy creatures she'd seen prowling the grounds outside were curling around the posts of her bed, peering out from behind the dresser, perched on the windowsill and watching.

They were right here.

In her room.

She rose slowly, searching for a weapon. How did one strike a shadow? Fear crawled through her, threatening to paralyze, as she thought of that attack she'd witnessed against the king.

But these shadows didn't attack her.

They seemed to be...*waiting* for her. Whispering to her. Just soft rustlings of noise and nonsense at first, but then they twisted, thickened into clear words: *What do you command*?

She gave her head a shake. She had imagined that voice, she was certain. And yet she heard herself answering it all the same: "I command you to *leave me alone.*"

The shadows scattered into dozens of smaller puffs of black. She watched them dart for cover, most eventually disappearing into the streaks of sunlight filtering through the room's curtains. Her breath left her in a slow, stunned exhale. It was a long time before she remembered to inhale—so long that she felt dizzy.

They had *listened* to her.

All save for one.

The largest of the shade beasts remained on the silk rug before her. It was rising to meet her like a serpentine dragon arching itself, preparing to shoot off into the sky, to take flight at her next command.

Sephia wanted to look away. Why was she still looking at it? It didn't have eyes, and yet she felt as if it was staring into her soul. As if it saw the Shadow magic buried deep inside of her, and it was being called by it.

This was dangerous.

This was different from the shadows Sephia had played with as a child. These were actual creatures. Sentient creatures that she had seen attacking a king, and that now apparently wanted to do her bidding—for reasons she didn't know. And if she used them, if they could somehow go after the prince...

But that is precisely what they need to do, isn't it?

She'd come here on a mission. She'd sworn to Nora that she would complete it by any means necessary. And here was a means, presenting itself on a silver platter.

It would be foolish not to at least make *some* use of it.

She took a deep breath. Steadied herself. The beast wanted a command, so she gave it one: "Go see what business the prince is up to."

Part of her still did not expect it to listen.

But it lowered itself—in a bow, almost—and then it slinked off, pressing underneath the door and heading into the hall.

Sephia watched it go with a sinking feeling in her stomach. She wanted to be cold, ruthless about the matter, but the truth was that the thought of spying on the prince suddenly made her feel... *sick.*

Sweat dotted her forehead. Her vision swam. She stumbled into the adjoining powder room, pumped water into the pedestal sink, and splashed several handfuls of it into her face.

Her vision finally cleared. She caught her breath, and then glanced at her reflection in the mirror above the sink.

And she realized, with horror, that her eyes had a blueish tint to them.

The witch's spell was fading much more quickly than she'd expected. More quickly than it *should* have.

"Perfect," she muttered to no one.

Never mind those unwanted feelings she might have been developing for the prince. The only feeling she needed to be concerned with was the feel of an executioner's blade against her neck—because that was *precisely* what she was going to be facing if she didn't get things under control.

The shade beast was gone. She couldn't control where it went now or what it did next, perhaps, but she could control what *she* did next.

She went back into her room and found that book Nora had given her, safe in the spot where she'd tucked it underneath the bed. She took the hidden vials from it and wasted no time mixing herself a reinforcing potion.

It was worse than the first dose she'd taken.

As she finished off the foul-tasting concoction, the room felt as if it was closing in around her. She dropped to one knee. Tucked her head toward her chest and tried not to pay attention to the way the colors and shadows and sunlight shifted around her, as this did nothing to help her already aching stomach.

When she finally managed to lift her head a few minutes later, she saw that another of those shadowy beasts lingered. It had taken on a feline-like shape, and it was stretching itself toward her, tilting its makeshift head in a studious way.

Worried about her?

She rose slowly and took a threatening step toward it. "You have to leave me alone."

The beast didn't move.

Sephia felt the claws of panic crawling for her again. Even if the Sun fae in this place couldn't see the shade beasts, surely they would sense that something was amiss if they kept lingering around her. The shadows couldn't stay.

I am not a bride of Shadows. I am the Sun bride. I have to be the Sun—

"Go away! Now!"

The beast retreated a few spaces, but it still did not disappear.

And Sephia could feel her buried magic starting to stir once more.

Keeping her eyes on the beast, she raced over to the nightstand and grabbed the discarded ring. Fumbled with nervous hands until she managed to slide it on.

"Stay down," she begged her magic through clenched teeth. "Stay *down*."

And it did.

With the ring back in place, her innate magic sank back down so violently that it felt like someone had punched her in the stomach. She wanted to double over and collapse in pain, but she stayed on her feet and kept her head lifted, her eyes trained on the beast until it finally wavered and then disappeared.

There one moment, gone the next.

But she could still sense it. Her magic was still reaching upward, trying to find it, making that ring on her finger burn hotter and hotter. The witch's potion continued to churn through her all the while, and suddenly everything, *everything* was too much, too painful, too sickening. The room reeled around her. She stumbled toward the bed. Reached for the edge. Missed it, fell—

She was unconscious before her head hit the floor.

CHAPTER 9

The members of Prince Tarron's small council all rose to their feet as he entered the meeting room, and all seven of them started talking at once.

"A shade beast of sorts—"

"Suspects in the city have been—"

"The Shadow Court—"

"Enough," Tarron snapped.

Silence sank over the group.

"Have a seat," he ordered. "And councilman Osric, please summarize what exactly is going on."

Osric nodded, and once they were all seated around the round table once more, the silver-haired man gave his summary: "Early this morning, one of the gardeners was found unconscious. When he regained his senses, he claimed to have seen a dark... *creature* of some sort before he fell."

"A shade of the belephor—an *umbra*," blurted out the council member to Tarron's right.

Councilman Osric silenced the interruptor with a cross look. "It isn't entirely clear *what* he saw; there were no other witnesses. But we sent guards to investigate, of course. And while searching the grounds for these alleged *beasts*, they instead stumbled upon two suspicious characters that we believe may have ties to the Shadow Court—though they've sworn otherwise.

"They don't carry the mark of the Shadow Lord, and their magic seems weak—too weak to conjure up any shade beasts, perhaps. But the supposed sightings of those beasts, coupled with potential enemy spies, makes for a...questionable situation. We've apprehended those potential spies, and we will interrogate them as you command."

The prince thought of the conversation he'd had with his brother the night before. Ten years since the original beast had slaughtered their parents. Three years since those beasts had last appeared in any form. Three years of *peace*.

He didn't want to see that peace shattered.

But after his brother's episode, and now that one of their servants had fallen too, they couldn't ignore this. What was causing these things, if not some form of those shadowy creatures?

They had never proven that rival court guilty of setting these beasts upon them. But if the ones they'd apprehended *did* turn out to be from Nocturne...

His blood chilled as he thought of the potential implications of such a thing.

And to think, he had started to tell Princess Leonora that these things could *wait*.

Why had he said that?

Why had he kissed her, for that matter?

It wasn't like him to give in to such impulses, or to make a show for the members of the court to gossip about. But there was no denying it: He'd *wanted* to kiss her. Desperately. Something in her voice had awakened a primal part of him that he'd long ago buried, and he'd wanted to claim her right then and there, brand her with his kiss, his touch, and for a moment he hadn't cared about whatever obligations he was ignoring or what any onlookers might have thought.

And while I was doing that, a war was potentially beginning in my realm.

He had let his feelings interfere with his duty, even though he'd sworn he wouldn't. And here he was, doing it again, losing himself in thoughts of her.

Chaos, she'd called herself.

An accurate assessment.

"Your thoughts, Highness?" prompted Osric.

Tarron forced his expression into something resembling calm, and he kept his tone hard and formal as he said, "You came for me, but where is my brother? Has he been informed of these matters already?"

"Yes." Osric hesitated. There was an unspoken question in his eyes as he continued: "The king retreated to his study shortly after we briefed him on the situation."

Tarron frowned, because he knew the question that Osric dared not to ask: Was Deven hiding away because he was feeling ill again? Concern gnawed at his insides, threatening to make his heart race and his voice shake.

Not now, he ordered himself.

He couldn't show that concern. Because if *he* looked concerned, then the rest of his council would follow suit, and panic would spread like wildfire throughout the Sun Court.

Besides, he'd shown enough damn *feelings* for one day.

"The two suspects," he said, "you're certain they're secured?"

"Yes. They've been taken to the *guest suites* down below. They're being treated to the highest level of security."

A quiet bout of humorless laughter echoed through the room; the king frequently referred to the dungeons as *guest suites*.

"Well secure them further," Tarron ordered, rising to his feet. "And I will see to them personally after I go and speak with my brother."

AFTER A BIT OF SEARCHING, he tracked his brother down —the king was no longer in his study, but in his private bedchambers. He didn't look thrilled to have company, but Tarron barged his way into the room and closed the door all the same.

Deven folded his arms across his chest, regarding his younger brother with a weary look. "You've heard about our little disturbance this morning, I'm assuming?"

"Yes." Tarron hesitated, choosing his next words carefully. "Though I should have been notified sooner."

The king shrugged. "You're normally strolling

through those gardens every morning; I was surprised to learn that you hadn't been there to personally witness the drama unfolding."

Images of the way he *had* spent his morning—laughing and cooking breakfast with Leanora, her voice mesmerizing him into kissing her—flashed through Tarron's mind once more.

Distracting, chaotic little thing.

He gave his head a little shake, as though that would rid him of the lingering feelings she'd stirred in him. "I was...otherwise occupied." Deven lifted a brow, but Tarron continued before he could say anything: "What about you? I thought you would be in the dungeons, overseeing the interrogation."

"I wondered if you might like to do it? You have more of a stomach for such things."

Tarron's eyes narrowed in suspicion.

"I'm feeling perfectly fine, if that's what you're worried about. I just have no desire to visit the dungeons today. You know the place depresses me."

"Osric is concerned about your health. I could see it in his eyes. I'm certain he said something about it to the rest of my council the moment I stepped out of the room."

"Yes," said Deven, offhandedly. "Osric says lots of things, and he speaks out of turn entirely too much for someone of his rank. We should work on remedying that."

"You could quiet them by taking care of this matter in a strong, decisive way."

The king brought his gaze level with Tarron's. It looked gravely serious for once. "Not today," he said.

"It must be dealt with."

"Yes, and you will go in my place, as I mentioned."

"Deven—"

"Leave me be."

Tarron did not move.

"That's an order from your king," Deven said, his tone cold and unyielding and so entirely unlike his brother that Tarron obeyed the order, backing out of the room mostly because he was too shocked to do anything else.

The dismissal didn't get under his skin until the door slammed shut behind him.

Why won't he just admit that he's getting sicker?

With one last furious look at the closed door, Tarron headed downstairs. He pushed his brother out of his thoughts. He considered only the task before him, making a list in his mind of what he would need to do to successfully interrogate their prisoners. A comforting, orderly list of things to check off. He was in control. *He was in control.*

He barely noticed a servant walking toward him until they nearly collided.

"Your Highness, a word—"

"Not now," he said, striding past without sparing a glance. But he made it only a few more steps before the servant found his voice and called after him—

"It's your bride, my lord."

Tarron rounded so quickly that the servant recoiled.

"What of her?"

"S-she's taken ill, I'm afraid. She—"

"Impossible." His heart leapt into his throat. "I was just with her. She was fine."

"The doctor thought you should be summoned." The servant lowered his eyes.

Tarron took a deep breath, averting his irritated gaze. He was angry at his brother, and at the day's strange happenings; no sense in taking it out on this servant.

"Very well," he said. "I will go to her. But I need you to deliver a message to Councilman Osric for me."

"Yes, of course—"

"Tell him to go warm our prisoners up for their official interrogation," said Tarron, already turning away and walking briskly back toward Leanora's room. "I'll be downstairs momentarily."

The servant said something in reply, but Tarron did not hear it; his pulse was throbbing too loudly in his ears, and he was moving too quickly.

He took the stairs to the second floor in leaps and bounds and then raced down the hall, slowing only when he caught sight of the doctor as he exited Leanora's room.

"What's happened?" he demanded.

The doctor gave a quick bow, and then he said, "One of the servants found her on the floor a short time ago. Unconscious."

Just like that gardener?

Were the shade beasts responsible for this too?

Tarron could not bring himself to ask the questions out loud—as if not speaking them would keep these horrors from being true.

But Doctor Elric wasted no time confirming his worst fears. "There was an enormous amount of magical...*residue* in the room when my assistant and I arrived. And it was not Sun magic."

The prince braced a hand against the doorframe. "And now?"

"It's settled now, and we've used counter spells to purify that dark energy. But the lady still sleeps. Her vital signs are stable, just weak; hopefully she is only drained, and with enough rest she'll recover soon enough."

"And you're certain of...of the energy you encountered when you arrived?"

The doctor's reply was quick and grimly certain: "I would guard her very closely."

Tarron exhaled slowly. "Understood."

His brother, and now his future wife...why did it all suddenly feel so much more serious? As if there was no way to deny they were being targeted. And those implications that had nagged at him earlier...

War.

That was what these things would mean, if the Shadow Court was indeed to blame.

He thanked the doctor and stepped into the room. A trio of servants finished up their tasks and bowed low before leaving him alone with his bride, and then he went to the bed, settled down on the edge of it.

For several minutes he sat in the heavy silence, watching Leanora's chest rise and fall to make certain her breathing stayed normal. He could still sense that dark, cold energy the doctor had spoken of. But it was faint now, and otherwise the room was strangely peaceful. His bride was safe. She was fine.

So what was he still doing here?

He could do nothing else for her.

The doctor and the servants were enough to deal with this matter. In the meantime, he needed to go deal with their prisoners. He needed to have a more productive conversation with his brother, somehow. He needed to tend to the reports on his desk, to speak with Councilman Osric and quell any rumors that the old man might be spreading...

He needed to do a hundred other things besides sitting there, uselessly, at his bride's side.

But the thought of leaving her caused an aching in his chest that made it hard to breathe, much less move.

So he stayed.

Against his better judgment, he stayed, and he eventually stretched out onto the bed next to her, lost in his thoughts. He didn't touch her. He wouldn't touch her while she was not awake to allow it. But he remained beside her for one hour, and then the next, as close as he could get without disturbing her rest. And though his magic was weak—because of the pieces of it still locked inside of her, ironically—he gave her what he could whenever she shivered or cried out in need of warmth or comfort.

Eventually he grew tired, drained from both magic use and the day's events. His eyes had just started to flutter shut when Leanora's hand struck out, clawing for something to hold on to. It found his hand. Wrapped it tightly. He didn't pull away. He should have, maybe, but he liked the weight of it against him.

It was infinitely preferable to the weight of all the things weighing on his mind.

Today had swiftly turned so...*disastrous*. And everything felt as if it was falling down around him. But the tighter she gripped his hand, the slower and lighter his racing thoughts became, and soon he found himself relaxing down into the pillow beside her, closing his eyes, and falling asleep.

CHAPTER 10

Sephia woke to the feeling of a rough tongue licking the hand she had dangled over the edge of the mattress.

"Ketzal," she mumbled, "that's disgusting."

She popped one eye open just in time to see the tiny griffin dive under the bed. He reemerged a moment later with a pair of fuzzy slippers in his teeth, which he shook at her. With a sigh and a sleepy smile, Sephia reached out and grabbed the slippers—and she realized in that instant that something was impeding her movement.

Someone had an arm around her waist.

She twisted around and saw... Tarron. Asleep in the bed next to her. Under the same blankets as her.

She didn't think, she just swung—*thwap!* went the fuzzy slippers against the prince's face, and then she was kicking, shoving him away from her.

He rolled out of her reach, catching himself just before toppling over the edge of the bed. He straightened up, blinked several times, and then glanced toward the window. "What time is it?" he asked, groggily.

Sephia drew the slippers back, preparing to strike again.

He held up his hands. "Okay, *stop*. This isn't what it looks like."

"Then what *is* it, precisely? Why are you in bed with me?"

"Put your weapon down and I'll tell you."

She kept a tight grip on the slippers but slowly lowered them to her side.

"Do you not remember fainting?" he asked, still eyeing her warily.

Her mouth opened... but quickly clamped shut again as she realized she didn't know what to say.

Her thoughts were a blur.

What *did* she remember?

Her disguise wearing off. The potion. The shadowy beasts watching her. Her magic, trying to escape, trying to tangle itself up with those beasts...

She didn't remember fainting, but her head was throbbing. There was an ugly bruise on her left arm, and that entire side of her body ached as if she'd fallen and hit the dresser and everything else on her way down.

Ketzal hopped into her lap and sniffed at the bruise on her arm. A gentle purr rumbled in his chest.

"I...I don't remember what happened," Sephia said as she ran her fingers over Ketzal's silky fur. "But I feel terrible."

The prince nodded, understanding. "I was worried about you. That's the only reason I stayed in here."

Worried.

The word sent a flood of feelings roaring through her —such a tumbling, confusing mess of them that she couldn't decide which one was the most accurate. All she knew for certain was that the room felt unbearably warm, suddenly, and that her mouth was too dry for her to speak.

"And I didn't mean to fall asleep beside you." Tarron raked a hand through his hair, and more to himself than her he added, "It was a long morning full of exhausting things, I guess."

After a moment of hesitation, Sephia tossed the slippers back onto the floor. She cleared her throat and said, "Sorry I hit you."

"You have an impressively strong swing for a human," he mused, rubbing the red mark she'd left on his cheek.

"Sorry," she repeated, feeling a bit sheepish now.

He waved the apology away. Climbed off the bed, went to the window, and drew the curtains back to reveal a red-washed sunset sky. He cursed softly under his breath—presumably because it had gotten so late. Turning back to her, he said, "This was a poorly-timed nap. I need to go, but I'll send servants in to see to you; if there is anything you require, simply ask for it. I'll be back to check on you myself later this evening."

She nodded in a dazed sort of way.

He left, and Sephia pulled Ketzal into her lap and continued to pet him while she tried to sort through her racing thoughts.

Soon, doctors and servants of all sorts were parading in and out of the room. She greeted them all with an increasingly tighter knot of terror in her chest—because they had to have suspected her at this point, didn't they?

They mostly spoke in their own confusing native tongue, but she distinctly heard them mention *strange, foreign energy* more than once. It was only a matter of time before they were able to trace that energy to her.

And then what?

Of all the obstacles she had been prepared to face in this realm, Shadow magic was not one of them.

Nor had she been prepared for the prince to be *worried* about her.

What was going on, precisely, and how was she going to keep it from destroying her and all of her carefully-laid plans?

Eventually, the doctor insisted she needed more rest. The parade of servants and such trickled to a stop. An hour passed without any intrusions, and Sephia finally decided that it was safe enough to crawl out of bed, go to the washroom, and study her appearance in the mirror.

That potion had worked again, of course.

An image of Nora was staring back at her. Such a perfectly-transformed image that Sephia could almost pretend she was back home with her twin, and that she could share all of these complications with Nora and then just stand back and wait for Nora's calmer, more rational mind to make sense of it all.

"This has become much messier than we'd planned for," she whispered, her heart heavy and aching as she reached out and pressed a hand against the mirror.

A *thud* and a quiet creak of floorboards sounded from the adjoining room.

Just Ketzal, she told herself.

Paranoia invaded her all the same. She left the washroom and walked along the edge of her bed chambers, searching. She paused by the window and looked out at that tower where she'd spotted the first shadowy creature.

But she saw nothing, and she *felt* nothing that suggested Shadow magic...

The ring the prince had given her was still on her finger, burning against her skin. She had become somewhat numb to that burning—though not to the oppressive, hot and heavy energy that it gave off. She twisted the ring from her finger and tossed it onto the nearest dresser. But the suffocating Sun magic still hung over her, no matter how much space she put between herself and that ring. Perhaps the doctor and his assistants had done something to the entire room?

I was worried about you.

So worried that maybe they were trying to protect her from those strange shadows, that *strange energy*, by using counter spells of their own. The irony of the situation was not lost on her, and fresh paranoia wound its way through her as she realized just how dangerously out of place she was in this court.

"No wonder I'm so tired," she muttered out loud.

Ketzal yawned in agreement. He leapt from his perch on the footboard of the bed and lazily glided over to her. He took her sleeve in his teeth and started to drag her back toward the bed, his tiny, slightly crooked wings flapping with all of their might.

It was all the encouragement she needed.

She flopped back down onto that bed, and before long, she had drifted off again.

SHE SLEPT INTO THE EVENING, and then on through the night. When next she woke, soft morning light was filtering into the room. Ketzal was curled up beside her, his mouth hanging open and letting little half-purrs, half-snores escape.

She sat up slowly. Despite her long sleep, she still felt drained and uncomfortable underneath that haze of Sun magic lingering in the room.

There was a knock on the door. The prince entered a moment later, carrying a tray laden with fresh fruits, breads, and an assortment of sweet and savory-smelling delicacies that she couldn't name.

"You didn't eat lunch or dinner yesterday," Tarron said, placing the tray on the nightstand. "I assumed you would be famished."

Her stomach twisted; she couldn't deny her hunger.

Ketzal could not deny his, either; he was airborne in an instant, diving for the center of that tray—Tarron caught him by the scruff of his neck and pulled him back at the very last second.

"And don't worry," said the prince, tucking the squirming griffin securely under his arm before turning back to Sephia, "I didn't cook any of it."

Sephia felt a smile tugging at the corners of her lips. "So no fires this morning?"

He returned her smile, though his didn't quite reach his eyes. "Not literal ones, anyway."

She was curious about what he meant, but he didn't seem to be in the mood to elaborate.

She let her gaze settle back on the food. It *looked* safe enough, and she had survived her last meal with him, hadn't she? She picked up two jam-drizzled pastries. She offered one to Ketzal—which he inhaled in a single bite — and then she nibbled cautiously on the corner of her own. After patiently waiting to make certain it would have no ill effects on her, she took another bite. The nibbling soon turned to gobbling with only slightly more restraint than Ketzal displayed.

She *was* famished.

They ate together with few words spoken between them. Sephia was surprised at how pleasant the silence felt.

When they had finished, the prince said, "The doctor suggested fresh air would be good for you. If you're feeling up to it, I could show you more of the grounds?"

She agreed eagerly; she was ready to escape this too-warm, too-heavy room that was starting to feel more and more like a magic-laced prison.

SHE CHANGED into walking attire and met Tarron at the main entrance, and they set off.

He allowed her to lead the way, and, after a bit of consideration, she decided to follow a path that wound its way up a hill and into what appeared to be a massive orchard. From a distance, the trees of that orchard appeared to glow with something other than sunlight; she had first spotted them upon her arrival to Solturne

Hall, and she'd wanted to get a closer look at them ever since.

The hill was steep. But it was worth the climb, because when they finally reached the top, the sight before them took Sephia's breath away.

The trees *were* glowing.

Each leaf was a different shade, from soft pinks to blazing oranges and reds, and they pulsed brighter and paler, brighter and paler, as though they each contained their own individual heartbeats. Shimmering dust filled the air, drifting and sparking around them like embers thrown from a fire. A heady, smoky sweet scent tickled Sephia's nose.

The trees were aligned in painstakingly neat rows, and she wandered from one row to the next, collecting different kinds of fruit and stuffing them into the pockets of her cloak. She intended to carry these spoils back to Ketzal.

Tarron rolled his eyes and muttered something about *spoiled beasts* when she informed him of this plan, but she was fairly certain he was fighting off a smile as he said it.

She continued exploring while the prince trailed slightly behind her. He answered all of her questions about their surroundings, but his answers were short and to the point, and soon he was glancing back at the palace they'd left behind.

"You seem worried," she finally said, circling back to his side. "And you mentioned *fires* earlier—not *literal* ones, you said. What did you mean?"

He shook his head. "Forgive me."

"Forgive you for what?"

"For not giving you my undivided attention. I shouldn't let the troubles on my mind distract me, I just..."

"You don't need to apologize." She hugged herself against the early morning chill. "Where I come from, we call that *being human*."

"Are you insulting me?"

She looked over and saw his lips quirking in the corners.

Joking around again?

He was, and it was becoming entirely too easy to smile back at him. She almost wished he would go back to smirking and being truly offended by everything she said and did—that had been easier to deal with.

"I only meant that you don't have to pretend around me," she told him. The hypocrisy of the words struck her as soon as she said them. She nervously tucked a strand of hair behind her ear and averted her gaze.

Tarron didn't seem to notice her inner turmoil; he clasped his hands behind his back and walked on. He was silent until they made their way to the banks of the slow-moving river that edged the eastern side of the orchard.

They wordlessly seemed to agree that this was a good place to take a break; Tarron leaned against a nearby tree, while Sephia stretched out on a flat slab of rock, removed her boots and stockings, let her toes skim the cold water.

"So..." she began after a moment "...are you going to tell me any more details about what's bothering you?" She wasn't entirely certain why she was pressing the matter. The words had just sort of...fallen out of her.

"It's all very boring stuff—politics and such."

"Perhaps I don't find these things boring?"

He hesitated. "You honestly want to know?"

"Yes."

He pushed away from the tree and came to sit on the rock beside her. "Well...we apprehended two criminals yesterday that we believe are tied to the Shadow Court. Either here as spies, or perhaps something worse."

"Worse?"

"We think they might be responsible for the strange magic some claim to have noticed around the palace. That this magic might be the cause of my brother's illness flaring up, *and* for the rough spell you went through yesterday."

Sephia's stomach gave a sickening lurch.

That's why the doctor and the servants didn't seem to suspect me.

They thought someone else was responsible for that shadowy energy.

And maybe they were? She didn't know enough about her own magic to say for sure. She had always kept it hidden, buried deep inside of her at her parents' insistence. She didn't even know what she was capable of. She had assumed those shadows were here because of her, but maybe they'd originated elsewhere, and then simply sought her out because like called to like?

"Is that a...common problem here?" she asked. "I thought the Shadow and Sun Courts had stopped their wars a long time ago. Middlemage serves as a mediator between your two realms, and things looked relatively peaceful as far as I could tell from the Central Palace."

"All true enough. But sometimes troublesome things slip through the cracks. Not everyone wants to keep our hard-earned peace. The Shadow Lord is young and ambitious. Hungry for more power, some say, at whatever the cost."

"You believe he wants to start another war?"

He started to reply, but then pursed his lips and seemed to rethink his answer. His voice was oddly strained when he finally said, "It wasn't long after he first took the throne that our city was attacked and my parents were killed. We never proved anything, but it's difficult *not* to suspect them when things like this start happening. They're different from us in many ways. And their magic is...darker."

"Darker?"

He nodded. "You must have learned something about it, given your twin and her innate Shadow magic?"

She pretended she hadn't, only because she couldn't bear to talk about that magic—*her* magic— out loud.

The weight of all of her lies felt exhausting, suddenly.

"Our magic centers around life and protection," said Tarron. "Theirs aligns with death and deception. Necromancy, shapeshifting, possession...perhaps I'm biased, but I can't think of a single *positive* thing their magic might be used for."

Her skin prickled at the harsh tone of his voice. She stared at the river, watched the water parting around her submerged toes.

He must have noticed her barely-suppressed turmoil this time, because he said, "Again: Forgive me. I didn't want to trouble you with all of this."

She shook her head. "No, I'm glad you told me."

He frowned, but after a moment he sighed and said, "It's better if you're aware, I suppose. Maybe it will help me worry less about you."

There it was again—that word.

He was *worried*.

About *her*.

She had been prepared to be a suspect. She knew how to fight, how to sneak in and out of places she didn't belong, how to hide her magic. But she was less certain of what to do about the fact that he was *worried* about her.

Especially since she was in control of the very shadows he believed threatened her.

She might not have summoned them, but she had ordered them away, hadn't she? It was the combination of the Sun ring and the witch's potion that had caused her to faint, not the Shadow magic.

What a mess I'm in.

She had come here to protect her sister.

Instead, she had become a spark that might inadvertently set a fragile peace ablaze.

Feeling suddenly restless, she stood and walked along the river's edge. She searched the clear waters for sparkling geodes, the way she and Nora used to do. She spotted a particularly round rock and reached for it.

A cold chill swept through her as she grabbed it and sank back onto her heels. She lifted her gaze to the opposite bank, and she immediately spotted the reason for that chill: *Another shade beast was watching her.*

She froze with the rock in her hand. She was wearing the prince's ring, and yet that beast was still there.

Could Tarron not see it?

It was small. Less solid than others she'd seen—just a wisp that soon swirled into a shape that resembled a weasel, long and lean and cunning, before it froze as well.

Once again waiting for a command?

The prince called her name.

No—her *sister's* name.

Images of Nora flashed through her mind, and she remembered, in that instant, what she had come to this realm to do. It felt almost as if the shadow had come to remind her of what she could *still* do. She was alone with the prince. Solturne Hall was no longer in sight. This shadow...could she command it? Set it upon the prince? She had done that as a child back home, after all, accidentally possessing that man when she'd needed to protect Nora from him...

Here was another potential *accident,* and isn't that what she'd planned for?

She only had to set things in motion. And then she could go home to Nora, and leave the fae world behind.

But at what cost?

She gave her head a hard shake. Turned away from the shadow. She could feel it staring after her as she walked back to Tarron, sat down beside him, drew her knees up and rested her chin on them.

"Don't worry about me," she said, softly. "What about your brother? How is he feeling?"

"Hard to say." The prince scooped a handful of stones up, skipped one across the water. "I'm worried about him, though."

"You're very close to him aren't you?"

He clenched the rest of the stones in his hand. Trying to crush them into a fine powder, judging by how tightly he gripped them as he bluntly said, "If anything happens to him, I will personally storm the Shadow Court and demand answers from the monsters there."

She thought again of Nora, of the things she would have done for her.

And she was realizing, however reluctantly, that she and Tarron were more similar than she ever would have guessed. Two young royals thrust into a situation that neither of them had particularly wanted, just trying to keep the peace and protect the things closest to them.

This was not how it was supposed to go.

He was supposed to have been a complete monster.

"You look deep in thought," Tarron commented after a few minutes of silence.

She tilted her head toward him, studying him, squinting against the sun rising at his back. "You just... you aren't what I was expecting, that's all."

"What were you expecting, precisely?"

Oh, what a dangerous question.

It took her a long, careful moment to think of a safe answer. "My life has been filled with stories of your kind, you know."

He arched a brow. "Do tell."

"All of the fae in all of the various courts have some things in common. They're...difficult. Easy to offend, fond of tricks, lovers of deadly games and cruel bargains. So many stories of...*beastly* behaviors. I thought my coming here was going to be the end of me, one way or the other."

Or the end of my sister, rather.

"Beastly, hm?"

"To put it mildly."

He laughed—that *stupid*, beautiful laugh. It seemed more pure, less guarded out here in the cool morning air, and so far away from the more proper places of Solturne Hall.

"In my defense," she said, "you acted beastly towards me more than once when I first arrived here."

"True enough." He was quiet for a moment before continuing. "And I suppose I *felt* a bit beastly yesterday, when I was kissing you."

"I asked you to kiss me and you did. You were a perfect gentleman."

"On the outside."

Her cheeks felt hot. "But on the inside?"

He cut her a sidelong glance. "Let's just say...I was not finished with you."

She swallowed hard. "And how would that kiss have finished, had we not been interrupted?"

He flung the rest of the stones into the river. "Not in the hallway."

Desire clenched the muscles of her lower stomach. She would have fought it off if she could have, but it felt inevitable, suddenly, as powerful as that water rushing past them.

"Because I suspect you would have wanted a bit of privacy while we fulfilled *that* particular part of our ancient bargain," he added in a voice that was soft, seductive, and sent every nerve in her body humming to life.

She stretched her legs out in front of her. Tried to

settle her nerves. She didn't trust herself to move any closer to him, but the way he was looking at her...

Was it possible he was beginning to want her for reasons *other* than that stupid ancient bargain?

Was it possible she wanted him too?

It was foolish. Dangerous. It could never work between them. If she strayed from her plan, he would find out the truth about her eventually, and it would likely mean death. And not only for herself, but for her sister, too.

Or perhaps...perhaps she could come clean? She could help him solve the mystery of these shadowy attacks, maybe. And then they could...

They could *what*, precisely? Marry and live happily ever after, as if they hadn't just spat on a treaty that had existed for generations? As if she hadn't been keeping a horrible, dangerous secret from him this whole time?

You're a fool, Sephia.

She knew this, and yet it did nothing to settle that desire pulsing through her.

"We aren't in the hallway anymore," she said, lifting her gaze to the sky.

"No. We aren't."

"And we're very much alone, aren't we?" She felt his gaze shift more fully to her. "And I'm feeling much better now that I've had a bit of fresh air."

"Are you?" His voice was even lower than before, husky with unmistakable *want*.

She looked down and found him watching her. His face was not closed off for once; the desire was written all over it. And he could have been a perfect beast about quenching that desire— she wouldn't have resisted him.

In that moment, she wasn't certain she *could* have resisted him.

He reached for her hand.

She reached back.

She wrapped her fingers through his. She let him pull her closer, all the way into his lap. Her knees settled on either side of him. She wrapped her arms around his neck and pressed her forehead to his. Closed her eyes. Their noses brushed, and then their breaths, their mouths, their tongues. His hands found her hips, steadied her as she rocked deeper into the kiss.

And slowly, slowly, slowly she felt something unfurling inside of her, felt the tightly clenched fist of all of her prejudices and misconceptions opening and her fears falling away as he held her more tightly, pulled her in closer.

The river rushed. The impossible future loomed. Those shadows may still have lingered nearby.

But for the moment, at least, she didn't care about anything else.

CHAPTER 11

*L*ater that morning, Sephia returned to her room to find more shadows waiting for her.

The room was *drenched* in them.

They roiled about, her own private tempest that seemed to mirror the storm of emotions inside of herself. Panic tingled through her, turning the tips of her toes and fingers numb. She closed her eyes. Breathed in deep. Tried to will both her inner storm and the outer shadows into submission.

When she opened her eyes again, it was just in time to see one shadow peel away from the rest. It slithered toward her like a snake unwinding, and with a start she realized that she recognized its shape, its specific energy —this was the one she had ordered to spy on the prince.

And now it was back, presumably to give a report.

Heart pounding in her ears, Sephia went to the door. Locked it. Double-checked the lock. Cautiously backed toward that waiting shadow beast, and then took another deep, steadying breath.

"Tell me what you know," she ordered, voice trembling slightly.

The shadows around the edges of the room billowed and collapsed, billowed and collapsed. A few pinched off from the larger masses and swept around her, whispering in a rapid and confusing chorus of different voices. Finally, one clear voice emerged, and it came from that serpentine beast directly before her: *He plans to kill them.*

It took Sephia a moment to comprehend. "The prisoners, you mean?"

The shadows tumbled more violently. They continued to whisper in chilling, distinct voices.

No trial, said one.

No mercy, said another.

No justice, hissed a third.

Kill him? begged a fourth.

Sephia's knees felt weak. She walked over and sank down on the edge of her bed, folded her arms around her stomach, and looked toward the door that led to the prince's room.

He wasn't in there. He had left her alone, yet again, while he headed off to tend to business.

The business of preparing for executions?

He hadn't told her any of that particular business while they'd been out for their walk. She should have pressed him about the matter more, perhaps. But she'd let herself get entirely too... *distracted.*

At least they had only kissed at the riverside. Nothing more than that. And she had been the one to pull away, even though she hadn't wanted to. She'd *had* to, and here was the reason for it, the reminder of what a fool she was to think she could stray from her initial plans.

Because whatever glimpses of decency she'd seen over this past week, she was fooling herself to think there could be a happily-ever-after for her here.

No trial, no mercy, no justice.

If he knew the truth about her, then he would kill her, too, wouldn't he?

"Leave me be," she ordered the shadows.

The whispers became more harsh, more rapid, more violent.

Kill him?

Kill him.

Kill him.

"No." The room chilled and darkened around her, as if the shadows were protesting, but she ignored them. She fought off a shudder and went to the window, drew the curtain back to let in more sunlight. "Not yet," she said. "I want to speak with him first."

THAT EVENING, she was waiting in the prince's room when he finally returned to it.

His eyebrows lifted at the sight of her. "Leanora —hello."

"You seem surprised to see me. Should I have requested an official meeting with you?"

"No." He frowned. Started to say something, but then seemed to think better of it and instead pressed his lips back into a smile. "No, you're always welcome in here."

Will I be welcome when you know the truth?

She was determined to find out. Eventually. *Eventually*, she was going to have to tell him that truth. But in the meantime, there was the matter of those prisoners. They might have been guilty of subterfuge, but so was she, and now she needed to know...

Would he show them mercy if she asked him to?

It was a test of sorts. One she had spent the entire day plotting and planning for.

"Is everything all right?" he asked.

"I was just...worried about the prisoners you mentioned this morning."

He snorted. "Worried?"

"What are you going to do to them?"

"Never mind that." He was carrying a stack of papers in his hands, and now he distracted himself from the conversation by walking over to his desk and dropping the papers onto it. After arranging them neatly next to a feathered quill, he turned to the shelf behind the desk and began searching and sorting through the books on it.

When he glanced back at her a minute later, he seemed surprised again—and perhaps a touch annoyed, now—to find her still staring at him expectantly. "You don't need to concern yourself with it," he insisted before turning back to the shelves.

"You wish for me to just look the other way while you deal out whatever brutal punishment you please?"

"You grew up in a royal court of your own, did you not?"

"I—yes."

"And that court, I presume, had its share of dirty deeds that needed to be dealt with."

She glared at him. Not that he saw it, as he kept his back to her.

"So you should have at least some understanding of how these things work." He paused just long enough to tilt his gaze toward her, and then returned to his searching and sorting. "We make examples out of the ones we've captured, and then the rest of them think twice about starting a war with us."

"Maybe they don't truly *want* war. If you could just allow them to talk, to—"

"Oh, but they *did* talk, after some persuasion."

"Persuasion?"

He didn't elaborate on how he had *persuaded* them. He only nodded and said, "And do you know what those bastards told me?" He withdrew several books from the shelf and dropped them onto the desk. Slammed them, really, and then he stepped around to the front of that desk and leaned back against it. "They said they had come for my bride."

Her heart sank horribly in her chest.

"So tell me, my bride, why would they come for you if they did not intend to start a war with me?"

Because I am Shadow, not Sun.

Did they know that, somehow? If they *did*, if they had come here because of her...

"I think you should at least give them a fair trial."

He laughed.

"Did I say something funny?" Her voice threatened to

shake, but she somehow kept it steady "Or is compassion and true civility a joke to you fae?"

He folded his arms across his chest. "I am being extraordinarily compassionate. If it was up to me, I would have already destroyed them both. Them and every last *trace* of Shadow magic in this realm."

Monstrous.

The word snaked into her thoughts, bringing all of her familiar, warm and comfortable prejudices with it.

Tarron narrowed his eyes. Pushed away from the desk and strode toward her. The movement felt almost like a threat. Or at least a warning.

She ignored that warning. "You're being unjust."

"As my wife, you—"

"Deserve to be heard," she snapped.

"Yes, well I've heard enough for one night. It isn't your place to worry about whatever prison scum we have rotting down below at any given time. You don't know—"

"Not my place? Then tell me, *my prince*, what is my place?"

He nodded curtly at the door behind her and said, "I think perhaps you should go back to your own room."

"I am not a child that you can just order to her room!"

He stared at her.

"I'm not leaving," she said, voice quiet but firm.

He closed more of the space between them. For a moment she thought he might grab her, shake her, try to rough her into submission. His eyes had taken on a strange glow, his fingertips had sprouted their claws, his movements were full of raw, barely-suppressed anger.

He *was* a beast, after all, and now she was dangerously close to pushing him over the edge.

But he stopped just short of reaching for her. He kept his hand clenched and at his side as he spoke: "What brought this on, truly?" The words were low and laced with incredulity, as was the humorless laugh that accompanied them. "Has it been too long since we've argued? Is that it? I was beginning to think we had turned a corner in our relationship."

"So was I," she said, unable to keep the bitter disappointment from her voice.

He seemed taken aback by that disappointment.

So was she.

But she couldn't deny it.

She realized then that she was upset not only because of his brutal treatment of his prisoners, but because she had started to believe—*wanted to believe*— that he wasn't a monster at all. That it wouldn't matter if she had Shadow magic. That he would understand her and the things she had done to protect her sister. She wanted peace. She wanted to be allies with him... No, she wanted to be *more* than allies.

And the realization that such a thing could likely never happen was crushing.

He stepped closer to her.

His stride was so confident, so powerful, that she unconsciously took a step back. Another step. Another, another, all the way to the wall, and then she attempted to sink into that wall.

Let me disappear.

We can't do this.

It can't happen.

But there was nowhere to go, and then he was very suddenly right *there*, bracing a hand against the wall on either side of her, and her body was responding with burning, traitorous desire.

"You try my patience, my bride," he muttered.

"I strive to challenge you."

"You succeed." He reached a hand up and cupped her face, trailed his thumb across her lips.

They existed in that moment for what felt like an eternity, poised on the edge of a fall that Sephia knew there would be no recovering from.

"I...I have another question," she finally breathed.

"Ask it."

"How do you feel about...*us*?"

A muscle worked in his jaw. "The laws—"

"I don't care about the laws that bridge our realms. I don't care about the bargain that was struck forever ago. What if these things didn't exist? What if I *wasn't* your stolen Sun bride, and I was...something else? Would you ever claim me as...as..."

His gaze moved across her face like a caress, lingering on her lips, her jaw, the pulse of her throat. "What foolishness is this?"

"Answer the question."

"You are mine." A simple, calm declaration. But just like his movements, there was power rippling underneath the surface of it.

She could scarcely catch her breath under the heat of his gaze.

"You are mine," he repeated, sending shivers

cascading through her entire body. "I stole you away from your kingdom because it was the expected thing, and I intended to carry out an obligation. But something's...changed."

"Changed?"

"I want you, and yes: I am beginning to think that I would *still* want you, whether all the laws in all the realms were for or against it. Is that what you wanted to hear? Is that enough to make you stop acting so strangely?"

Mine.

She wanted to believe it.

But the voices in her head were relentless—

Don't be a fool, Sephia.

This can't work.

The shadows lingering in her room were proof, such painfully devastating *proof* that this could not work. And yet she was still staring into the prince's eyes, transfixed by the possibility of things.

The possibility of *them*.

"You are one of the most chaotic, confusing beings I have ever met," he continued, roughly, "and if I was smart, I would send you back to your room and lock you inside it." His eyes closed. His forehead leaned into hers. He didn't kiss her. He just stayed there for a moment, breathing her in.

"I'd like to see you try to lock me anywhere," she whispered, her lips nearly brushing his with the words.

Her challenge coaxed a quiet laugh from him, sent it spilling, warm and electrifying, across her lips. "I'm not going to try," he said.

"Smart."

"Not as smart as I *thought* I was before I met you. On the contrary—I'm a damned fool if ever there was one."

The words emboldened her. Or made her stupid. She still wasn't certain which, but for whatever reason, her reply was quick and daring: "If you are a fool for me, then why don't you prove it?"

"Damnable woman." His smile was more of a baring of teeth as he brought an arm around her waist, jerked her body flush against his. "I don't need to *prove* anything to you."

"Of course not. You can still send me away."

He kissed her instead.

His lips crushed against hers, hard and unyielding. His tongue soon followed, demanding entrance. When she didn't immediately yield, sharp teeth found her bottom lip. She thought she tasted blood after the bite, but for some reason that only made her desire burn hotter. She swayed with the weight of that desire, and his hand was against her hip in the next instant, holding her with a strong grip, guiding her back against the wall.

Her eyes fluttered shut. Pinpricks of light swam in the darkness before her. This felt different from the gentle, slow kiss they'd shared by the river. It felt darker. Hungrier. As if his day had been full of dangerous, poisonous things, and he thought that kissing her deeply enough might cure him of those poisons—or at least help him endure it.

She was dizzy by the time he finally pulled back.

She reached up and pressed a hand against his cheek. Partly to brace herself. Partly because she wanted to feel the rough stubble of his jaw, the strong, sharp lines of his face.

He *wanted* her, he'd said.

And though he'd claimed he didn't need to prove this, it had certainly felt like that last kiss was trying to prove something.

She wanted him to do it again. To prove it over and over, until she believed in it completely. Until she was confident enough that they couldn't, *wouldn't* be shattered by that ugly truth she needed to tell.

"No more running off to take care of any other business tonight," she said.

"I'm a busy man," he countered. "If you intend to keep me here, I will need to do something productive, at least." His eyes danced with wicked intent. "So what *business* shall we tend to?"

She ran her tongue across her suddenly dry lips. "Take off your coat."

He did as he was told, tossing it onto a nearby chair. And he didn't stop with the coat. His eyes stayed locked with hers as he slowly, deliberately unbuttoned his shirt and then shrugged it away, revealing hard ridges of muscle that she longed to touch.

He could see that longing in her gaze, judging by the smirk that played across his lips.

He didn't tease her any further.

He stepped forward and claimed her lips with his own once more, and while his tongue explored the soft shape of her mouth, her hands explored the firm lines of his stomach. Her fingertips traced lower and lower. He moaned into the kiss, deepened it as he found the ribbon at the nape of her neck, the flimsy tie that was holding her shirt in place.

He untied it.

The shirt slipped down, the soft material pooling at her breasts. His mouth moved to the newly-exposed skin, kissing a trail along her shoulder, up the curve of her neck, pausing to nibble on her earlobe.

She was braced against the wall, but even so, she felt as if she might crumple to the ground if he kept moving his lips across her ear like that.

He lifted her off her feet before she could.

He carried her to the bed. Laid her down and then hesitated at the edge of the mattress, worshipping her with his eyes rather than his lips and tongue for a moment. Giving her a chance to reject him, maybe.

She should have rejected him.

She didn't.

That raging storm inside of her...it was back again. It kept her moving. Searching. Seeking shelter within his embrace. It made her reach for him, and then pull him closer when he took her hand. His pine forest scent enveloped her, and the weight of him settling, sinking her deeper into the mattress made her feel safe. Protected. *Wanted.*

He kissed her again, and what little bit of space existed between them sparked with sudden, magical heat.

Sun magic is life-sustaining, protective, warming...

She inhaled sharply at the memory of his words, at the unwelcome reminder of this magic that was so incompatible with her own.

He stopped kissing her. Braced his hands on the sheets beside her and drew back—though he didn't go far. His mouth hovered just inches above her own as he asked, "What's wrong?"

"Nothing, I just..."

I just need to tell you the truth.

She exhaled a slow, shuddering breath. She meant to exhale more words with it. But she was a coward in the end, and she said nothing.

He leaned a little farther back. Studied her for a moment. "You don't have to rush into this," he said. "I know the whispers and stares of our court have bothered you, but they make no difference to me. We can wait. On this, on the wedding—on all of it."

The thoughtful crease of his brow only made her want him more.

But he was right. This was too rushed. And too unfair, given the secrets she was keeping. But she couldn't go back to her room. She couldn't be alone with those secrets. Those shadows.

She finally found her voice: "We shouldn't rush. But I...I don't want to go back to my own bed tonight."

He rolled over and stretched out beside her. She slowly followed him, moving so they were side-by-side, facing each other, knees touching, hands brushing, fingers lacing together.

After a moment he reached up. Brushed a few strands of hair from her face. Let his hand linger against her cheek. He was looking at her as if it was the first time he had ever truly *seen* her.

And she had a wild, reckless thought: She wished the

potion she'd taken would somehow spontaneously wear off. That he might blink and she'd be changed in that instant, and then he truly *could* see her.

"I don't want to go," she repeated, softer.

He pressed closer for one last slow, gentle kiss.

"You don't have to go anywhere," he said.

And she began to wonder what it might be like if she never had to go at all.

CHAPTER 12

*S*ephia did not return to her own room until the following afternoon, at which point she and Prince Tarron went their separate ways. He had to go meet with his brother, and though he invited her to come along, she declined.

Because while he was otherwise distracted, she had her own plans to carry out.

She dressed quickly, muttering to herself as she mentally rehearsed the plans she had spent most of the night and the morning deciding on.

Ketzal was perched on the headboard of her bed, watching her, head cocked to the side. He made a noise deep in his throat—half purr, half whine.

Worried, it sounded like.

Before she left, she paused long enough to walk over and scratch his feathery chest one last time. "If this goes poorly, just know that I'll miss you," she said. "Stay here and stay out of trouble, okay?"

And with that, she headed downstairs.

She moved with the confidence of someone who knew where they were going. Someone who belonged in these halls. It was largely an act, as so much of this past week had been. But after today...

If I survive today, I won't have to act anymore.

It had all been an act in the beginning. She wasn't sure at what point that had changed— when she had gone from pretending to be the prince's bride, to actually *wanting* such an impossible thing.

But she had not been pretending last night, when they had kissed so deeply.

The fluttering, happy feeling that had overtaken her when she'd woken up beside him had not felt like a lie, either.

That feeling was worth chasing, she'd decided.

And it was that feeling that kept her moving. She wasn't entirely sure where she was going. She only had a vague idea of the palace's layout, thanks to several conversations she'd had with servants— but she knew she needed to reach the prison hold, and she assumed it was located on one of the lower levels.

So she simply kept heading deeper and deeper, and eventually the light and splendor of the halls above gave way to darker, emptier spaces below. Soon after, she was met with an earthy, damp smell that suggested she was on the right track, and she picked up her pace.

Two guards spotted her as she came to the bottom of a particularly winding set of stairs. They moved to block her path, exchanging a slightly confused look before offering her a bow.

"My lady," said one—a silver-haired, much older-looking fae who she assumed was the leader and the more experienced between the two of them. "How can we help you?"

She saw rows upon rows of keys hanging on the wall just ahead—cell keys. She was in the right place, it seemed.

"My bridegroom wishes for me to speak with the two prisoners that were recently apprehended," she lied. "He wasn't satisfied with the initial interrogation of them, and I am here to follow-up on some things."

They exchanged another look.

"Alone?" asked the younger guard.

Her reply was quick and confident: "I was involved in similar duties back in my home kingdom, and I intend to make this duty a permanent part of my service to *this* realm. And I would like to begin it today, if you would kindly step aside."

"Princess Leanora, surely you know we can't—"

"It was the king's idea." If she was going to lie, she might as well commit entirely, she figured. "Do you wish to go against *both* the king and the prince's wishes?"

A long pause. And then the lead guard frowned and said, "Give us a moment, will you?"

Sephia nodded. They stepped away, and while they conversed amongst themselves, she searched for something to distract herself with, something to keep from fidgeting or otherwise looking guilty.

A flicker of movement in the corner caught her eye. She sensed that cold, clinging energy, that pull on her buried magic that was familiar by this point.

She squinted toward that movement. And as she

expected, she saw another of those living shadows that had become her near constant companions.

It was sitting at the edge of an arc of torchlight, watching her. Like an eager-to-please dog waiting for a command. No—more like a fox, with pointed ears and a thick, swishing tail.

She instantly thought of several useful commands she could give. She was getting too comfortable with these shadows, perhaps, and it was too risky...

But one glance in the direction of those guards made her heart sink—she could tell by their frowns that they still did not intend to allow her to pass, and no amount of *discussion* would likely change their minds.

She had to change their minds.

She couldn't fail. She had to get inside the prison and talk to these alleged Shadow fae criminals face-to-face.

So her eyes narrowed on the fox beast, and she mouthed out a simple command: *Send them away.*

The shadow obeyed. It leapt up, bounced off the wall and propelled itself toward the silver-haired guard. It landed on the guard's shoulder. Wrapped around his neck like a scarf and then sank into him, a spirit taking up residence in a stolen body.

Sephia kept thinking her command: *Send them away. Away, away...* Just as she'd done as a child, when she had accidentally possessed that man who had been harassing her sister. She had sent him away, too.

Away, away, away...

The guard shuddered. Paused. Shook his head, as if trying to shake out a nasty thought. Both of the guards turned back to her, and for a terrifying moment Sephia thought they would realize what she had done. She still could not believe that she *had* done it, that such a powerful trick had come so easily to her.

But it had.

And the elder guard's eyes were glazed over when he returned to her, and his words slurred slightly as he said: "We'll leave you to your business, then. Be quick about it."

The second guard shot him a confused look. This was clearly not the decision they'd agreed upon.

But he didn't argue with the one in charge, and Sephia hastily thanked them both—before either had a chance to catch on to what she was doing.

She hurried away. Another set of stairs awaited just around the corner, darker and yet more winding than the last. She couldn't see the bottom, but she snatched a lighted torch from the wall, picked up her skirts, and began her descent without hesitation.

Down and down and further down she went, while visions of the past days weaved in and out of her thoughts—

The first time she had heard Tarron laugh.

The first time he had kissed her.

And the latest kiss they'd shared just this morning, tangled amongst the sheets and each other, the morning sunlight warming their skin and their hearts beating in the same slow, steady rhythm.

She had never felt the way she'd felt this morning. Or the way she'd felt last night when they'd lain side-by-side and he'd told her she could stay.

He had wanted her to *stay*.

And not because she was a pawn. It was not about bargains or laws. It was more than that.

They were more than that.

Somehow, they had become more, and now she had to set things right. She had to get to the bottom of this mystery surrounding the dangerous shadows that had overtaken this court, even though it might mean revealing all of her own lies in the process. And if he didn't want her after that, she would understand. But she couldn't keep pretending. It was too dangerous. Too selfish. She had to make up for those lies, somehow, and then maybe...

She steeled herself. Gripped her torch more tightly, and continued her search. There were at least a dozen cells stretching along the hall she'd reached, and only a few of them appeared empty.

She started to panic, wondering how she might find the ones she was looking for. But then she felt it, that cold breeze of magic stirring deep inside of her, trying to catch her attention.

The shadow fox that had overtaken the guard had returned; it bounded onto the path in front of her, turned several circles, and then set off into the dark.

She followed.

It led her all the way to the end of the hall, to a small alcove that contained a cell set apart from the rest. It slipped through the bars of this cell.

Sephia moved after it without thinking. She was so busy trying to see where it had gone that she was startled when a body slammed against those bars.

She stumbled back, thrusting the torch out in front of her, brandishing it like a weapon.

There was no one there to strike.

The body had already retreated into the dark—but she knew it was still there, just out of sight, because she could still hear it. Its ragged breaths were the only sound she was aware of for several moments.

She gathered her courage and choked out a command: "Show yourself!"

No response at first. But then she heard shuffling movement, and though nobody appeared, a deep voice spoke from the dark: "So the Shadow princess has decided to pay us a visit."

Sephia threw a glance over her shoulder, eyes scanning the darkness for any guards who might have followed her in despite her tricks. When she was certain she was alone, she stepped closer to the bars once more. "How do you know who I am?"

The being on the other side of the bars began to laugh.

A second being joined it a moment later.

"Stop that," she hissed.

They stopped.

"I am trying to figure out the cause of the dark happenings in the palace above," she said, "and I might very well be able to help you escape in exchange for your cooperation. So I am going to ask you one final time: *How do you know who I am?*"

She didn't truly know that she could—or *would*—help them escape, but she had to say something to make them believe she had leverage over the situation.

"Well?" she pressed.

Another dark chuckle echoed through the cold air. And then the voice finally gave an answer: "I am your sender."

The words sent a chill winding through her, even though she didn't understand them.

"Sender?" she whispered, nervously swapping her torch from one hand to the other. "What does that mean?"

"You honestly don't know who you're dealing with, do you girl? I thought you would have figured it out by now." The voice had changed. Suddenly it was no longer deep and cold, but wispy and sickeningly sweet, like...like...

No. It can't be.

"Come closer to the bars," Sephia ordered. "Step into the torchlight so that I might see you more clearly."

The being obeyed. It came so close that she could have reached out and touched it. Her gaze swept over a tall, lean body. Dark eyes. Dark hair. Tapered ears, a sharp smile, a sharper gaze that made her breath catch as it settled on her.

Then shadows started to rise from its skin. And as they engulfed its body, that body began to *change*. To shift and to shrink into a hunched figure with long white hair, piercing blue eyes...

And suddenly the being staring back at her was familiar.

It was the same witch who had given her the potion in the woods.

Sephia took a step back as her hand flew to her mouth.

Our magic centers around life and protection...theirs aligns with death and deception. Necromancy, shapeshifting, possession...

"Shapeshifter," she breathed. "Shadow fae."

"As are you, in your own way."

Sephia shook her head and grabbed the bars before her, fighting the urge to sink to the ground underneath the weight of all of her mistakes.

How could she have been tricked like this?

"But the witch of the woods," she stammered, "she was not fae. She—"

"She left long ago, despite what yourself and the other residents of Ocalith have been led to believe. She's been gone for nearly eighteen years, in fact."

"Eighteen years?"

"Since soon after you and your sister were born."

Her skin crawled as a dozen realizations and dark possibilities sprang into her mind.

"I haven't been there for eighteen years, mind you," said the Shadow fae. "There have been several of us over the years, watching you. Waiting to see if we could make something useful out of you."

"Hiding in the woods like *cowards*, you mean?"

"We had to be close enough to help you with that magic you were born with, didn't we?"

"Help me? What did you *do*? What did I..." She felt dizzy, suddenly, as she thought of all of those strange, shadowy moments she'd experienced growing up. Her magic had always seemed stronger than most of the Shadow twins that had come before her, the palace elders said. More wild. And there were those rumors that her magic was responsible for awful things, like...

"Nora." Her sister's name left her in a painful gasp. "Is it true that my magic was responsible for her sickness? Did you have something to do with that?"

"It could have been a clean accident," said the fae in a voice that was smoky and smooth and entirely unapologetic.

The other fae remained in the shadows. Its mad laughter occasionally echoed through the space, but otherwise it contributed nothing but more uneasiness to the conversation.

"But you proved...resistant to our control," said the one standing before Sephia. "So she lived. Shadow cursed, but still living. A lot of our kind gave up on you after that. But I still saw potential, so I decided to pay you a visit. And I soon discovered that you planned to take your sister's place, and so I..."

"You used me."

"*Helped* you."

She squeezed the torch in her hand, barely resisting the urge to jab it through the bars.

"We are on the same side, Sephia," said the fae, calmly. "And you've gotten exceptionally close to the Sun Prince, just as you told me you would. So you can still help us."

She could hardly spit the words out quickly enough: "I won't do it."

"No?"

"I share your magic. Not your enemies. I won't fight

those enemies or restart whatever wars you want to with this court."

"I see." The fae wrapped its fingers around the bars of the cell. Leaned closer. "But you still want to protect your sister, don't you? More than *anything*?"

"Yes, but—"

"You're too far into this to stop now. If you tell the prince the truth, he will kill you. And then he will take his armies and storm Central Palace, and he will kill your sister and the rest of your family, too."

Her breath caught.

"You had a plan when you came here. You were so *certain* of that plan when you came to visit me in the woods. Your hatred for this court and its prince was so deliciously palpable. Deep down, I know that hate still burns. And this is why I've told you the truth now, just like you asked me to—because we are allies."

She shook her head and took a step back.

"You don't belong here, Sephia."

"I *could*."

The still-hidden fae laughed louder.

"The Shadow Lord would owe you a tremendous favor if you helped us," said the one half-illuminated by her torch. "And then, of course, you could come home with us afterward."

Home.

"You don't belong here, little Shadow princess. Help us, and then come back with us to Nocturne, where you could flourish. Where people don't fear you like they do in Middlemage. Where you don't have to shroud yourself in lies like you do here."

The offer enveloped her like a tight embrace. She was tempted to sink into it, to close her eyes and let it carry her away. It was magic at work, and she knew it.

But she couldn't shake it off.

Not until she pictured Tarron's face. His eyes blinking open with the sunrise, and the slow smile spreading across his face as he saw her....

Her answer came quickly after that.

"No." She was terrified, but she repeated herself all the same: "No. The Sun Prince is not my enemy."

"We'll see, I suppose." The Shadow fae bared its teeth in a grin. He was staring at something behind her.

She took a deep breath and turned around.

Prince Tarron was standing there, flanked by the two guards she'd tricked into letting her down into this prison.

And all three of them were looking at something in the corner of the room—a shadowy cloud that was swirling, shifting, separating into four stout legs, a muscular body, a massive head with powerful, snapping jaws.

It was far larger than the beast Sephia had controlled earlier. More solid. It felt too powerful to be overlooked, but she still hoped against hope that it might somehow still be invisible to their eyes.

"What is *that?*" asked the younger guard.

"*Umbra,*" said the other, quietly.

Prince Tarron did not speak.

Mad laughter rang out from deep in the cell.

"Better stop it before it attacks him," whispered the Shadow fae at Sephia's back.

The beast lunged.

Prince Tarron stumbled back, drawing the sword at his hip—a sword that Sephia doubted would have much effect against the charging beast.

She didn't think beyond this, she only reacted.

Her magic rushed through her, violent and desperate to call out to the shadow beast, to match that cold energy it was made of. To draw that energy toward her, somehow.

Like calls to like, she thought, desperately. *Pay attention to my magic!*

The moment her magic successfully intertwined with the beast was jarring—like she had leashed it, but she wasn't strong enough to keep her feet when it lunged forward. She thought she might be ripped apart from trying. But she held on, stumbling several steps before finally managing to dig her heels in and keep still.

Stop, she ordered the beast. *Stop!*

And the beast finally stopped. It curled back to her before bursting, scattering into smoky wisps of black that seeped into the cracks along the stone floor.

The prince lowered his sword.

Sephia dropped to one knee, exhausted by the effort the magic had taken. Her entire body ached.

"You...controlled it," said Tarron.

"Yes," she whispered.

But the cost of doing so was immediately evident in the wide-eyed and furious expressions on the guards' faces.

Tarron's expression was far worse—not fury, but confusion. And then... *hurt.*

"I was going to tell you the truth," Sephia said, her gaze dropping to the ground. "I swear I was, I just needed to...to..."

His guards converged, stepping between him and Sephia.

He didn't stop them.

They roughly grabbed Sephia's arms and hauled her to her feet, slamming her back against the bars of the cell. When her ears stopped ringing from the pain, and she finally managed to lift her head, it was just in time to see Tarron turning away from her.

"Lock her in the eastern tower," he said. "She can await her trial there."

CHAPTER 13

*T*here was nothing the prince could do.

Solturne Hall was in an uproar. Less than an hour had passed since the incident in the dungeon, but the true identity of his stolen bride had already gotten out. He hadn't thought to tell his guards to be discreet about securing her in the eastern tower—he'd been too angry to think.

So they had dragged her across the palace, essentially in plain sight. Someone had seen, or perhaps that younger, inexperienced guard had spread the news himself. Who knew? Who cared?

All that mattered was that the news was out, and there was nothing Tarron could do to take it back.

Nor could he take back anything that had happened between himself and Leanora—or whatever her name was—over these past days.

He raced up the steps to his brother's room, his heart beating a painfully furious rhythm in his chest. He nearly knocked over the guards stationed at the king's door in his haste to push his way inside.

The king was in front of the freestanding mirror in the corner of the room. He saw the reflection of his younger brother, and he offered a nod as a greeting before walking over to the wardrobe, grabbing his crown from the cushion on top of it, and putting it on.

"So," he said, turning back to study his reflection in the mirror, "we were tricked."

"You already know?"

The king's face tilted toward a servant gathering up linens and piling them into a basket against her hip.

She averted her eyes and hurried out of the room when Tarron narrowed his gaze on her—off to gossip some more, most likely.

"News travels fast," Deven commented, dryly. "I don't know how much of it is true, of course."

"The princess controls shadows."

"Yes, that was one of the things I heard."

"And that much *is* true. I saw it for myself, as did two of the dungeon guards. She obviously isn't who she claimed to be."

"She was disguised, somehow?"

"It seems so."

"That explains her strange scent, I suppose."

Tarron nodded, feeling like an even bigger fool than he had in the dungeon. He had noticed that strange scent, too—before they'd even left Middlemage. And he had suspected her that first night she arrived, when she'd acted so strangely in the gardens. She had seen shadows then, too—he would have staked his life and reputation on it. She had obviously watched them attacking his brother. He had *asked* her about it, even.

But she hadn't told him the truth, and he'd let it go, and now...

"So what now?" Deven asked.

"She will stand trial alongside the Shadow Court spies we apprehended."

"And what are we charging her with, precisely? Was she spying alongside them, you think?"

"No, but—"

"She controls shadows, but did she use them against us?"

"I don't know for sure. But even if she hasn't, it doesn't mean she *wouldn't* have, if we hadn't caught her."

"She didn't do this to me," said Deven, holding up a hand that shook slightly in spite of his obvious efforts to stop it from doing so. "You realize this, right? This curse was laid long before she ever arrived."

"We don't know that her being here didn't help aggravate it."

"We don't? I thought you two were growing quite close...do you really believe she would have purposely attacked me? Or you?"

No.

The word came instantly, empathetically to mind.

But that was his heart speaking. And as a general rule, he didn't listen to his heart. He listened to his brain. Or he always had before, anyway— until all of this arranged marriage nonsense.

He had always been the more logical one, compared to Deven. And perhaps it was only because he didn't want to think about that raw pain that had torn through his heart earlier, but he doubled down on that logical side of himself now. "She might not have done it on purpose," he said, "But those Shadow Court members obviously intended to use her, and she went to them this afternoon without consulting me first. It was reckless at best."

"Perhaps."

Nonchalant as always.

It only made Tarron angrier.

"I wonder why she lied?" Deven mused, leaning closer to the mirror and adjusting his crown.

"Does it matter?"

"It does if you intend to pass judgment over her. I am not in the business of baseless executions, and neither are you. Also: I know you care about the reason. It's written all over your face."

Tarron didn't reply right away. He wanted to argue, but he couldn't—because he *did* care. He didn't want to. He hadn't *intended* to. It would have been so, so much easier if he had stuck to his original plan of not letting his feelings get in the way of his obligations.

"Do you think she trusts you enough to give you an honest confession at this *trial* you're planning?" Deven asked.

The prince frowned—because he doubted it.

And now that one doubt had gained a foothold in his thoughts, a flood of others soon followed it.

He could have done better, perhaps. Not left her in the dark about so many things. But he'd wanted to think of her only as weak and in the way, and he had done his best to push her away for most of the days they'd spent together—so that he wouldn't risk those damn *feelings* that had ended up complicating everything anyway.

So no, she likely didn't *trust* him.

Maybe if he'd given her more of a reason to trust him, she would have told him the truth, and they might have found a way to fix things.

But that didn't matter now.

"I will make her confess, one way or another," he said, quietly.

"Will you?"

"Yes. Because she put our realm at risk."

"True enough." Deven let the words hang in the air.

"She *lied*."

"I know. And that is unforgivable, isn't it?"

Tarron didn't dignify this with an answer; he was tired of playing this game. He didn't want to leave this room until he had calmed down, but he didn't want to meet his brother's expectant gaze, either, so he went to the window and pulled the curtains aside, searching for something else to focus on.

He could see the eastern tower from here. His false bride was locked inside of it, as she deserved to be. It couldn't be changed. It *wouldn't* be changed.

She had *lied*.

But then again...

She had also stopped that beast from attacking him, hadn't she? And he could picture her face very clearly, that exact moment he'd seen her true magic revealed.

She had looked devastated.

As devastated as he'd felt.

Voluntarily recalling the memory of that devastation

was like stabbing himself in the gut and twisting the knife around. Further proof that he had started to feel something for her, in spite of his every effort to avoid this.

In such a short time, she had somehow found a way in.

She had made him laugh for the first time in what seemed like forever, and she had made him forget about bargains and duties and obligations. Earlier today...he'd just wanted to be with her, regardless of tradition. Because for a moment, yes— it had felt right. *They* had felt right.

But his feelings toward her were irrelevant, now.

He had to make them irrelevant, because dwelling on them would only mar his judgment. There was a duty to be carried out. And if his brother would not carry it out, then he would have to do it himself.

Even if it hurt.

CHAPTER 14

*S*ephia spent two days locked in a room that was scarcely larger than a closet.

She barely slept. She barely ate. The guards stationed outside of the door were the only other living things to interact with, and they had apparently taken vows of silence, because they would not speak to her no matter how many questions she asked or what demands she made.

She felt completely and utterly alone.

Her thoughts were her only company, and they were not kind.

As she awaited her fate, she tried to piece together all that had happened. Tried to make sense of all of those pieces. But no matter what explanations she settled on, it all came back to one simple, ugly conclusion: *What a fool I've been.*

She had spent so much time convincing herself that Tarron and his court were monsters, had been so blinded by her own prejudice, that she had not realized she was making her *own* monstrous mistakes.

And now she was not going to get the chance to fix those mistakes.

Her tricks were fading away. She was transforming back into her true self. The potion was wearing off—again, more quickly than she'd been led to believe it would. Perhaps it was because of the heavy, suffocatingly warm Sun magic that hovered over this place. Occasionally, she heard extra movement outside of her room—spellcasters at work, she thought—and soon after, she would feel a rush of that awful magic that countered her own. It felt almost like the members of this court were trying to cleanse her with it, to make her sweat out all traces of Shadow magic in her blood.

It wouldn't work.

She was still the Shadow sister, and what a mess she'd made by pretending to be somebody she wasn't.

She was curled up on the cold floor, wrapped in a single thin blanket. Every ugly thought she had made her fold a little more tightly into herself. She wished she could curl tightly enough to disappear all together. Numbness started to overtake her thoughts and her body.

Then she heard a familiar voice outside.

She sat up and hastily reached for the glass of water one of the guards had left, and she gulped it down and tried to clear the dryness in her throat. It had been so long since she'd talked to anyone that it felt as if any words might splinter her throat on their way out. And she had so, *so* much to say.

Though something told her Prince Tarron wasn't going to want to talk anymore.

The door to her prison opened, and he stepped inside.

"I-I'm glad you're here," she stammered. "We need to talk."

Their eyes met. She thought she saw a flicker of uncertainty in his. Or regret, perhaps, for locking her away like this.

But all he said was, "It's time to go."

"Go?"

"The main council has decided to try you separately from our Shadow Court prisoners. That council is waiting for you now."

"Oh. Right."

She knew it was coming, but still some foolish part of her had hoped he might change his mind. That they *all* might change their mind, and she wouldn't have to answer for what she'd done.

So foolish.

Two armed guards arrived to escort her. Her hands were bound, and then the four of them made their way outside, down a narrow set of stairs that led to a large circular room at the tower's base. Here they joined a group of more guards and servants—an entire procession to lead her to her trial at...well, she didn't know where. It didn't matter. She wasn't thinking about where she was going. She was still too caught up in the places she'd been, thinking about all the things she could have done differently.

The prince walked several paces ahead of her to start

with, speaking with one of the servants. But as they reached the first floor of the palace, he slowed his step and fell in beside Sephia. With a curt nod, he dismissed the two guards that had been personally escorting her.

At least a dozen feet now separated them from anyone else in their procession. Not exactly enough room for a private conversation, and yet it somehow felt like only the two of them existed now, for better or worse.

He didn't speak right away. He seemed to be bracing himself for whatever he needed to say. The hurt and anguish were written plainly across his face once more, as painful as they'd been in the dungeon the other day.

He didn't look at her as he finally spoke. "Your name is Sephia Anne Caster. Not Leanora."

She fixed her eyes straight ahead. "Yes."

"You had the *audacity* to insist on having my true name when we first met, and yet you did not give me yours."

She didn't reply.

"I have spent the past two days collecting all of the information I could about this *Sephia*. I've also written a detailed letter to the Middlemage court about what has transpired, though it remains unsent."

"You've been busy," she said, softly.

"Yes." A long pause, and then: "And I've been researching Shadow magic, as well. I already knew the basics, of course. But I have been trying to figure out the rest."

"And what did you figure out?"

"Those other fae we captured...I believe their intentions were to use you as a vessel, a conduit of sorts. With you in the palace, close to myself and the king, they didn't have to actually be within the palace grounds themselves. They've confessed to sending shadows that they hoped you would be able to use. Shadows that you could see, I'm assuming?"

She fixed her eyes on the ground while she nodded.

"And that you controlled in some cases? That first evening in the garden..."

"No," she replied, quickly and honestly. "I saw shadows around your brother that evening, yes. But I didn't do anything to make them attack him."

At least, not on purpose.

But a terrible possibility occurred to her then: Could she have been using that dark magic without even meaning to?

Was that how Nora had gotten sick in the first place?

She thought of both Nora *and* the Sun King, of the way their illnesses mirrored one another's. And there had always been rumors that Sephia was responsible for her sister's sickness, hadn't there? She had always told herself that such a thing was impossible, that she never would have hurt Nora, but what if...

It should have been a clean accident, is what that imprisoned Shadow fae had said.

They had tried to kill Nora at birth—this had obviously been their original plan to destabilize the Sun Court. And they had used Sephia as a vessel for their magic back then, too, sent the shadows through her to do their bidding.

"There's more," said Tarron.

She cut her gaze toward him, afraid of what he would

say, but desperate to listen all the same.

"I have a theory that your magic may be powerful enough that it draws any dormant Shadow magic to the surface. My brother was attacked years ago by shade beasts, but survived. He has been sick ever since, but functional enough—until these past weeks. His struggles started to resurface in earnest once we collected you from Middlemage. So even if you did not purposefully set your shadows upon my brother, your being here was still destined to make a mess of things."

She shivered, clearly remembering the words Prince Tarron had said that day at the riverside—

If anything happens to him, I will personally storm the Shadow Court and demand answers from the monsters there.

From monsters like her.

But another thought occurred to her then, though she was too numb to speak it: *What if I could draw it all the way out?*

She had always been taught to suppress her power. But what if she embraced it? What if she could control that Shadow sickness deep inside of the king, same as she had exercised control over the shadows that had been haunting her since she came here? What if she could draw it out, like poison from a wound, and then send it away?

She wanted to believe that there was still a way to make things right. And that perhaps...perhaps she was no more a monster than anyone else. Perhaps the line between monsters and mistakes was very thin, and what she chose to do next was more important than anything she'd already done.

"Answer one thing for me before we reach this trial," said Prince Tarron, quieter now.

She tilted her face his direction, and she saw that he was finally looking at her.

"Why did you do it?" he asked.

She took a deep breath.

And she finally told him the truth.

"I did it to protect my sister," she said. "I thought this court would be a danger to her, but I was wrong. Wrong about you. About everything, really. And I... I'm sorry. And if you would give me a chance to do it, I swear I would find some way to make it right."

All of the hurt, all of the anguish in his expression was suddenly gone, and his face became an impenetrable wall. His gaze moved back to the hall before them. He was quiet for a long time.

"Tarron—"

"The council will decide your fate," he finally said.

They exchanged no more words after that.

Eventually, they reached a pair of massive doors that each featured a deep carving of the Sun Court's emblem. The throne room, she was fairly certain. On the other side of these doors, her jury awaited.

She was out of time.

She would never know what Prince Tarron was thinking in that moment. She would never know if there was some way she might save the king, or Nora.

Gods. Nora.

She would never see her again. She had made too many mistakes. She had failed.

And now it was time to face the consequences.

CHAPTER 15

The king sat upon his throne in the center of the room, flanked on either side by five servants.

He looked terrible, Sephia thought—as if they had dragged him from his death bed and propped him up with sticks on that throne. His skin was pallid, his eyes glazed over. She could feel the shadowy energy snaking through him. But she didn't have an opportunity to focus more fully on it before suddenly there were hands upon her arms, yanking her forward, distracting her.

To the right of the throne was a row of elder fae, standing side-by-side, all of them dressed in grey robes with drawn hoods. The silver-haired one in the center—Councilman Osric, she believed his name was— held what looked like a gold-plated lamp with a Sun etched into its side.

She was forced to kneel before them.

Tarron walked over and stood by his brother.

The servants then left the king's side and went to the tall windows spaced evenly along the sides of the room. They drew the dark curtains over those windows aside, flooding the room with sunlight. Councilman Osric said something in the language of the Sun; he spoke slowly and clearly enough that she thought she understood the basic meaning of it—

Now we shine a light on the truth.

A tingling sensation of magic followed the words, and Sephia shuddered as it settled over her skin.

Her hands stayed bound behind her. Two guards approached with a black strip of cloth, and they tied it around her head, blinding her. She sensed several more guards circling around her. Heard swords scraping free of sheaths, and—she assumed—being pointed in her direction. She could almost feel the sharpness that hovered just beyond her reach, daring her to make even the slightest move.

There was perfect stillness for a moment, and then the Sun King cleared the frailness from his throat and forced out a single, booming word: "Proceed."

And so her trial began as she knelt there, suffocating under the warmth of sunlight and magic, blinded, knees digging into the cold marble floor, heart heavy with regret.

But Sephia only partially paid attention to the crimes being read, just as she had only partially paid attention to the details being recited on the day of her Taking.

Because just as she had that day at the bridge, she was busy going over plans in her head.

She might have been out of time and terribly low on options, but she had already decided that she would not go out quietly. She was reaching out with her senses, focusing in the direction of the king, trying again to feel that shadowy magic he'd been poisoned with.

Like calls to like.

If she could feel it, if she could call it, take hold of it....

There.

Her body was suddenly cold, not warm, as a violent wave of Shadow magic shot through her. Her body trembled with the effort of trying to absorb it, nearly toppled over, and she was once again snatched by the arm and jerked back into place.

Frigid steel was at her neck a moment later.

She held in a gasp.

The steel dug in, and she felt blood bubbling up and sliding down her throat, shockingly warm against her magic-chilled skin. She swallowed hard and closed her eyes—a reflexive response, in spite of the covering over them—and she sank back into herself and tried to return her focus to the king.

She had almost recovered when a harsh voice broke through her concentration: "And so we have the guilty verdict," declared Councilman Osric.

Guilty.

"Now for the sentencing."

Her attention snapped back to the reality of the moment, and the hold she had on the king's buried shadows slipped once more.

They reached that verdict entirely too quickly.

"You have a plan for this punishment, I assume, Your Highness?"

"Yes," said the king.

Sephia tried again to go back to her plans. But her heart was pounding too hard, and her breaths were coming and going too rapidly for her to think about magic anymore. So she kept perfectly still and listened as the king finally continued, in a quiet but powerfully focused voice.

"I do," he said, "But I don't believe it is my place to hand out this particular sentence. She was to be the bride of my brother; the lies she's told have affected Prince Tarron the most, and so I believe he should be the one that decides her punishment. And whatever plan he has for her, it has my full support."

Rough hands jerked Sephia to her feet.

She held her breath, and it made all of the sounds around her suddenly louder. Footsteps coming closer. The sound of another sword being drawn. The whispers of the council and all of the servants and guards surrounding them.

Sephia braced herself for the feeling of a second sword against her neck.

She hoped it would be over quickly.

She hoped the Sun Court would at least be kind enough to not tell her family the full details of this moment; Nora would not be able to bear such a thing.

She closed her eyes tightly once more. Imagined herself someplace far away—back in the woods with Nora, climbing that great sycamore tree, the honeysuckle-scented wind blowing the waves of their hair about.

She was at peace.

She was slipping away already.

And then she heard the prince say: "I still plan to marry her."

CHAPTER 16

*S*ilence.

The room went so still that Sephia felt off-balance, unable to see and now unable to hear anything that might have helped ground her. The moment felt suspended, surreal.

What was going on?

A blade slipped between the bindings on her wrists. Pulled slowly, carefully, and then suddenly those bindings were falling away.

As they hit the ground, she finally remembered to breathe.

Gentle hands fumbled with her blindfold, and then it was gone as well. She blinked slowly. Let her eyes adjust to the change in lighting. Reminded herself to keep breathing as her vision cleared and she found herself face to face with the prince.

Noise was building all around them. Whispers. Objections. Arguments. She wasn't listening to any of it. She was lost to the world outside, just staring into

Tarron's eyes, and he was staring into hers, and all she could think was...

He had *chosen* her.

All of her life, she had been the Shadow twin—the dark one, the feared one, the ruthless one. That was who she was, and how she had arrived in this place, and how she had planned to leave it.

And he *knew* that, now.

But somehow, he didn't care.

He was the sun, but he wanted to be with her in spite of her shadows.

"I know it isn't the way of things," he said, voice low and meant only for her. "But before you arrived, it's...it's like I was sleeping. I wanted nothing to do with any of these feelings, or any of this *chaos*. Not until you. You woke me up. " He took her hands, pulled her closer. "And I would forgive every mistake, undo every law, and break every tradition, before I chose to go back to sleep without you."

There were a thousand things she wanted to say and do in that moment. Apologies, declarations, questions.

She wanted to kiss him.

She wanted to hold tighter to his hands and drag him out of this room, out of this palace.

In the end she only kept still, because it was enough to just be there for a moment, drinking him in, letting the words he'd said settle over her like a warm blanket wrapping around her, keeping her safe.

"It's *Shadow magic,*" she heard someone snarl. "She has obviously used it to possess our prince and his mind, to make him make such questionable choices."

Tarron's grip on her hands tightened. "They won't touch you, whether you are a questionable, *chaotic* choice or not," he told her. "Don't worry."

But she wasn't worried.

An odd peace had overtaken her.

"I need to do something," she whispered, and she pulled out of his grip, left him staring after her with a mixture of concern and confusion in his eyes.

That peace inside of her wobbled a bit as she turned and started toward the king. Dozens of angry gazes followed her every movement. But she managed one step, and then another, and then she was halfway to the throne, and then closer still—close enough that she didn't have to raise her voice to make it carry to the king.

"I want to help you," she told him.

The king's gaze dropped toward her. His hands, grey and shaking, gripped the arms of his throne more tightly. He seemed to be struggling to focus on her face. And before he could reply, guards filed into the space between them, forming a wall, blocking Sephia's path.

Sephia took a single step back before she caught herself. She steeled her resolve and held her ground, keeping her eyes focused on what she could still see of the king through the wall of armor and weapons before her.

A tense moment passed.

Then came a cough, and then the king's voice: "Let her come closer."

A few of the guards shuffled uncertainly, but most kept still with their hands resting uncertainly on the grips of their weapons.

"I said *let her pass*," coughed the king.

Slowly, a few of the guards peeled away.

Sephia stepped forward, and as she passed through the wall of sentinels she breathed in deeply, relaxed fully into her senses once more. She let her eyes flutter shut, and she soon felt it, just as she had when she was blindfolded—the cold ribbons of Shadow magic snaking themselves around the king.

Now I just need to draw them out.

Just as before, her body shook with her first attempt.

"Sephia, you don't need to do this."

Tarron's voice. It sounded like he was very far away. But something told her he was closer than he sounded— a feeling she couldn't name, a pleasant warmth—and a small smile curved her lips at the thought.

Strength surged through her. She reached again for the shadows, and this time she managed to keep still when they began to strike and tug at her senses. She imagined them as actual snakes, and in her mind she began to unwind them. To untangle them. To draw them toward herself.

She blinked her eyes open and saw the king slumping forward as the shadows spilled from his body. He was eerily still, as if those shadows had been his bones, his very framework, and now she'd drained him of all stability.

The thought was horrifying, and she was not the only one who had it, apparently; guards were suddenly rushing, arguments were building all around her, it was chaos—

Until it wasn't.

That same peace from before overtook Sephia. She couldn't explain it, but she was not afraid. All of the noise in the room settled into silence. She saw lips moving, people rushing around her. But all she heard were the whispers of those shadows she had drawn out. All she focused on were the threads of darkness weaving around her. She was standing in the middle of these threads, and they were encircling her, eventually blocking her view of everyone else.

She *should* have been afraid.

But she wasn't.

She didn't care about the toll this might take on her. She didn't care what happened after this moment—she would face whatever it was. Right now, she only wanted to help the king. To prove to Tarron and anyone watching that she was not a monster, and that she could and *would* atone for her mistakes.

The dark threads wound more tightly together, encasing her in a deeper, tomb-like darkness.

She lifted her hands. Slammed them back toward the ground, and watched the shadows slam toward that ground an instant later.

Leave us, she thought as they struck the marble.

They dissipated with a noise like a clap of thunder, rattling the windows and shaking the chandeliers and stealing Sephia's breath on their way out.

All that remained were little wisps of black. Several of the council members sprang into action then, flooding the room with Sun magic, and Sephia watched the lingering traces of shadows suffocate underneath this power. One by one they all disappeared, and soon she could see the king once more.

He lifted his head. His eyes looked clear, his hands no longer shook. Their gazes met.

Sephia inhaled and exhaled a slow, weary but satisfied breath.

And then she was falling.

Strong arms caught her. Cradled her. *Tarron.*

She was warm and safe now, and her job was finished, so she closed her eyes and fell asleep.

SHE WASN'T sure how long she blacked out for. But when she finally managed to open her eyes, she was still in the same place, staring up at the coffered ceiling of the throne room.

Still in Tarron's arms.

His touch was warm, her blood was cold, and it felt as if they were balancing each other out. As if all of the world was finally balancing out.

"Is your brother okay?" she heard herself mumble.

He nodded and gathered her more completely against his broad chest. Kissed the top of her hair, but said nothing; she thought he might have been too overwhelmed to speak.

She managed to lift her head and crane it in the direction of the throne, and she saw the king still sitting upright, speaking to one of his guards.

"*Reckless,*" snapped an elderly voice from somewhere behind her.

"Be quiet, Osric," Prince Tarron snarled back.

King Deven rose to his feet and spoke before their argument could continue. "Let's settle this now."

He braced a hand against his throne for a moment. Only a moment. Then he stepped down from the platform that throne sat upon, his movements as powerful and confident as Sephia had ever seen them. He cleared his throat and said, "As far as I am concerned, this woman is not a criminal. She is not who she claimed to be, and by rights she had no business being here, walking our halls and making a mockery of long-standing bargains and traditions. *But—*"

A chorus of anxious whispers began to rise throughout the room.

He held up a hand, silencing them.

"But days ago, she protected my brother from a potentially deadly attack. And now she has selflessly put herself at risk to take care of me as well."

"But a sentence must be carried out if we—"

"Sentence? Did you not hear what Prince Tarron said earlier?"

Every gaze in the room was suddenly upon Sephia.

She somehow found the strength to get to her feet. She and Tarron stood side-by-side, hand-in-hand, listening.

"It seems as though she will be marrying my brother." He glanced at the two of them as he made this declaration, and he winked. "And that," he added, "is punishment enough, I believe."

EPILOGUE

One Week Later

Sephia sat on a bench made of stone, surrounded by rosebushes.

This patch of garden had quickly become her favorite spot amongst the sprawling grounds of Solturne Hall, and for good reason. The view was unmatched; the white stone and gold-accented face of the palace itself was centered behind her, while in front of her was a wide, perfectly manicured trail that led out of the gardens and swept up to the rolling hills in the distance. The sun was setting over those hills, drenching them in a rich, glowing shade of orange. All around her, bees buzzed. Birds chirped. A warm breeze blew, and Ketzal bounced from one stone bench to the next, trying to catch butterflies.

It was as peaceful and perfect as a place could get,

Sephia thought as she stretched and laid back on the bench.

And the letter she had clutched against her chest made it all the more perfect.

She had written to Nora several days ago, and earlier today, one of the palace servants had finally brought her Nora's reply.

She unfolded that letter and held it above her, reading over it again, tracing her fingers over the words her sister had penned. Her touch paused on the last line—

I can't wait to see you again.

She was going to see her again.

Finally, she could relax. Nora was safe, and she would be coming to visit soon. And once she was here, Sephia would heal her as she had healed the king, and then her little sister could stand by her side at all the important moments they were going to share throughout the rest of their lives, starting with...

Her wedding.

It still did not feel entirely real.

And there were more details to figure out, of course, but she wasn't worried about them. Whatever happened now, it felt like she was heading into a happily-ever-after that had seemed impossible just a few weeks ago.

She refolded the letter and slipped it into the pocket of her coat. Laid her head down on the solid stone, let her hair cascade over the sides of the bench—her dark, natural waves of hair—and closed her eyes.

Minutes later, she heard footsteps approaching. She popped one eye open just in time to see Ketzal spin in mid-air, abandoning his butterfly chasing as he propelled himself toward a new target. He landed first on the end of her bench, and then bounded along it, bounced off of her stomach and launched himself into the air.

"Ow," Sephia said, laughing even as she grabbed her stomach.

"I warned you about his manners at the very beginning of this," said Tarron, catching the catapulting griffin and wrangling him into a secure hold.

"You did, didn't you?"

Ketzal wriggled about until he succeeded in getting the prince to scratch his ears, and then he purred happily, slipped free, dropped to the ground, and went back to hunting bugs and butterflies.

Sephia smiled as Tarron leaned down and kissed her. First her forehead, and then he braced an arm on either side of her and pressed his lips against hers. He pulled away slowly, and she sat up, feeling a little dizzy—both from the kiss and the change in orientation.

"I'm going to work on those manners," she declared, her smile drooping a bit as she watched Ketzal digging around one of her favorite rosebushes.

"If you are able to train him, I will be more impressed by *that* than by anything you've done yet."

She arched a brow. "You doubt me?"

"No." He chuckled softly. "I know better than that by now."

She smiled and scooted closer to him, wrapped her arm through his. "How did the negotiations go?"

They hadn't executed those two Shadow fae prisoners. After much discussion and debate, they had instead decided to use them as bartering tools, negotiating a peace agreement in exchange for their release.

Sephia had stayed by Tarron's side through several long nights of drafting the documents that they'd eventually presented to the Shadow Court. Delegates from that rival court had arrived for discussion just this morning, and though Sephia could have stayed for those in-person negotiations, the letter from Nora had arrived and distracted her.

But she fully intended to be a part of these politics in the future. As they both embraced her Shadow side more, she hoped that it might lead to a more peaceful existence between the two courts, and she wanted to help lead the way in any way she could. She was now Shadow and Sun *and* human, essentially, so who better to play this role?

"The new treaty is officially signed," Tarron told her. "Hopefully it will last for a little while, at least."

She gave his arm a squeeze. "If it doesn't, we'll deal with whatever comes."

He kissed the side of her head as she laid it on his shoulder. "Yes," he said. "I believe we will."

And that was that. Just as before, Sephia felt as if there were obstacles looming and questions unanswered, but she could face all of these things so long as she was by his side. It might be a messy version of happily-ever-after, but she was still ready and willing to fight for it.

Her eyes had started to close, relaxed as she was to be tucked so securely against him, when a distant sound—a popping and then a sizzling—caught her attention. She lifted her head and stared at the sky, and after a moment there came an encore of those sounds, accompanied by the sight of bright streaks of light that formed all manner of symbols against the falling curtain of twilight.

"What is that?" she asked.

"Fire writing. It's a traditional magic display during our bonding ceremonies. They're practicing."

"It looks beautiful."

"Yes," he said. But he wasn't looking at the skies when he said it; he was looking at her. She blushed, and he angled his gaze back toward the sky. "The whole court is officially starting to get excited about this wedding, I believe."

"The king is, certainly," Sephia said, grinning. "He keeps popping into my room and asking for my opinion on everything from flowers to chair coverings."

"He's just excited for an excuse to throw a party."

They shared a quiet laugh.

"If it's too much, we can always run away and elope," she said, more seriously. "I would be okay with that, just so you're aware."

"You know, weeks ago, I would have agreed with that idea in an instant." He looked back to the fire and smoke filled sky, a dreamily content look upon his handsome face. "But now I think they might be on to something—we should celebrate."

Sephia's expression brightened once more. "I agree."

"So bring on the decorations."

"And the drinking?"

"And the dancing."

"And the presents?"

"And the feast."

"Okay, but one rule about that last one."

"And what might that be?" he asked.

"You aren't allowed to cook any of that feast," she said, and then they were both smiling, laughing even harder than before, and he leaned in to kiss her as the shadows around them intertwined with the light of the setting sun.

The End

Don't miss the next STOLEN BRIDES OF THE FAE book!

COLLECT THE ENTIRE STOLEN BRIDES
OF THE FAE SERIES!

Read these books in any order for swoon-worthy romance,
heart-stopping adventure, and guaranteed happily-ever-afters!

You can find them all at www.stolenbrides.com

A NOTE FROM THE AUTHOR

Hi reader! Thank you so much for reading this short and sweet little tale! I hope you enjoyed reading it as much as I enjoyed writing it.

If you're looking for more books by me that are longer, steamier, and just all around more epic in scale and content, you can check out my latest series, the Shadows and Crowns series, which begins with The Song of the Marked. It has the same amount of humor and heart as Stolen Shadow Bride, but there's significantly more dragons, more cursing, more people getting stabbed with swords, and just more questionable content in general (but like, the fun kind of questionable content).

Whether you pick up any more of my books or not, thank you so much for giving this one a shot. Readers like you are the reason I get to do what I love for a living, and I could never put into words how grateful I am for that. I hope you'll check out the rest of the Stolen Brides of the Fae books as well, and do consider leaving a review if you enjoy them!

Sincerely,
    S.M. Gaither

You can keep in touch with S.M. Gaither in her VIP Group on Facebook.

ACKNOWLEDGMENTS

Another book down, and, as always, there are lots of people to thank for it!

Firstly, thank you to the rest of the Stolen Brides ladies-- Emma, Sylvia, Tara, Angela, Clare, Kenley, and Sarah. You all amaze and humble me with your talent, professionalism, and just all around awesomeness. I'm so grateful that I've had the chance to work on this series with you!

To Amanda Steele with Book of Matches Media, thank you for all you've done to help us get the word out about this series! And also for putting up with me.

To my ARC team and my V.I.P. Reader Group for your enthusiasm and support for this little side project--and all of my books! You all keep me going on the hard writing days.

And finally, to Grant, the inspiration behind most of the happily-ever-afters that I write.

Made in the USA
Columbia, SC
31 May 2021

38404112R00133